Mrs. C. A Westbrook

The Pilgrim and other Works

Mrs. C. A Westbrook

The Pilgrim and other Works

ISBN/EAN: 9783743305045

Manufactured in Europe, USA, Canada, Australia, Japa

Cover: Foto ©Andreas Hilbeck / pixelio.de

Manufactured and distributed by brebook publishing software
(www.brebook.com)

Mrs. C. A Westbrook

The Pilgrim and other Works

MRS. C. A. WESTBROOK.

The Pilgrim:

AND OTHER WORKS.

ST. LOUIS:

PIERROT & SON, PRINTERS.

1886

DEDICATION

TO the Youths of Texas, I dedicate this, my first work, hoping it may assist them in climbing life's rugged hill. And that the good old book " PILGRIM'S PROGRESS" may possess some attractions in its new dress, I have tried to cull fair flowers from the best writers, and arrange them in a bouquet which I pray may send forth rich fragrance to gladden each heart. Of one thing they may be assured: There is no thorn of sophistry concealed to pierce the soul. I seek not to derive pecuniary profit from its sale. My purpose is to appropriate the proceeds to beneficent purposes.

Your friend most truly,

MRS. C. A. WESTBROOK.

PROEM

THE radiance of Bunyan's star was resting on my heart
When forth its worship came, unbid—of life a very part.
The brightest day from darkest night is sometimes seen to
spring,
And captives oft, 'mid prison's gloom, the sweetest anthems sing.
And as I sat in silence bound, and sought the wondrous goal,
The worship—faint at first—became, the passion of my soul.
New peace and love with hope and joy, in holy beauty blend,
And yet I tremble to the world my little book to send,
For some will frown, and some will smile, and others look askance ;
Some will peruse, some ha'f read o'er, while others deign a glance ;
But if the Father doth approve the offering of His child,
His loving benediction grant, and bless her with His smile,
'Twill prove reward enough to bless for hours of thoughtful care
And onward to the " promised rest" her hastening footsteps bear.
Oh grant, Dear Father, in this book, as in a mirror bright,
Our youth may see the narrow way that leadeth up to light,
And learn to shun within themselves, the faults which they condemn
When brought to view as " blight and blast" in lives of other men,
Inscribing on the inmost heart the precept " Know thyself "—
Esteem above Fame's passing breath or cankering hoard of pelf
The soul God-given, which shall outlive the utmost bound of time
And rise to greet the Cherubim and join the hymn sublime.

THE PILGRIM.

→∷ AWAKENING. ✝ DEPARTURE. ✳←

OH thou now borne on Fancy's eager wing,
 Back to the season of life's happy spring!
 I pleased remember, and while memory yet
Holds fast her office here, can ne'er forget,
Ingenious dreamer, in whose well-told tale,
Sweet fiction and sweet truth alike prevail.
Whose humorous vein, strong sense, and simple style
May touch the gayest, make the wisest smile.
Witty, and well employed, and like thy Lord
Speaking in parables his slightest word,
I name thee not, lest so despised a name
Should move a sneer at thy deserved fame.
Yet, now, in Life's late autumn day,
That deftly crowns my brow with silver gray,
Revere the man whose " Pilgrim " marks the road
And guides the " progress " of the soul to God.
Oh poet, sad the effulgent beam
That lighted cell, and shone in dream,
Burned in thy heart, inspired thy pen
And made thee great, 'mid fellow men.
The goddess Wisdom never sped her dart·
More grandly, nor with more skilled art,
Than when she rent the Dreamer's night away,
And turned his darkness into healthful day.
But, now methinks I hear you say
You've slightly wandered from your theme away.
Thus Bunyan wandered through the world, it seemed,
And while he wandered, thus, the Dreamer dreamed;

A man he saw, a wretched one,
Forlorn, in rags, unpitied and undone,
Standing alone, within a certain space ;
A book was in his hand, and on his face
An anxious look, upon his back a burden bore,
His straining form was turned afrom his door.
Opening the book, with trembling dire he read ;
And as the truth burned in his soul, in dread
Cried out, with loud and piercing cry,
" What shall I do, Oh, whither must I fly !
I'm filled with sin, death's doom is o'er my door ;
I dare not rest me here, I know not where to go !"
Then, coward as he was, he hushed his deep distress
Lest his deriding wife would mock his wild unrest.
Silent he could not be, for stirred conscience strove,
And of his former sins a death-pall wove.
Louder he cried, " Oh! who can me relieve
Of this great burden. Who my soul retrieve!
My friends, this city will be burnt with fire.
The God of justice will his risen ire
Vent on you all, unless you now repent.
Oh flee, oh flee, at this His message sent."
His friends deriding him, with jest invoke
Morpheus to lull him, and thus avert the stroke,
But night as daylight, doth its horror keep,
And thought's dread spectres haunt the deepest sleep.
The day's dark clouds had settled over our hero's mind ;
At night the thunder came ; he cried : where can I find
Relief? What shall I do—oh, tell me—to be saved?
And tortured thus, he loudly, madly raved.
With prurience rude one asked, " Say, wherefore dost thou cry ?"
" Oh friend, this book informs me I'm condemned to die,
And after death to judgment I must come,
And there receive the sinner's hopeless doom,
I cannot do the first, I cannot bear the last,
My life is full of anguish, and yet I hold it fast."
EVANGELIST. " If this thy case, oh man, why standest thou stock still ?"
THE MAN. " I know not where to go. Oh, why did Satan fill
My cup so full of woe!" A roll to him he gave and bade him haste
      to fly.
" Seest thou that gate? If not, you steadfast fix your eye
Upon that shining light which you can clearly see.

When at the gate, loud knock and it shall opened be."
He swiftly set to run. His wife aloud did cry.
No heed gave he to her, but with unswerving eye
Bent on the cherished goal, entreaty he did spurn.
"Eternal life I seek, I dare not now return."
Ne'er looking back he sped him onward through the plain,
With sinew stretched and body bent, he pressed the gate to gain.
His neighbors mocking came, and two of them by force
Would bring him back, for, with the wife they said, "he crazy is, of
    course."
The name of one was Pliable, the other Obstinate.
"Why come you, friends?" the runner cried. "To save you from the
    fate
You rush to seek. You're crazed, poor one." "Not so, I have my head,
Destruction is your city's name. You dwell among the dead,
I'm just from there myself, my friends, and this I know full well,
Unless you hasten 'long this way, you'll sink with it to hell!
Go, go with me, I beg of you. Oh, heed my earnest call."
"What! go with you?" said Obstinate, "and leave behind our all?
We're sent for thee to bring thee back, but seeing you are bent
To go your way, forsaking all! Whence comes this sharp intent?"
"I go," said Christian, "to a land where peace and joy abide ;
No clouds are there, nor winter's storm. No good is there denied ;
Bright flowers shed their fragrance sweet, o'er all the heavenly air ;
No fade is there, no sorrow's tear ; but gladness everywhere.
In seraph's lay, I too, may join, in that blest home above
Whose sun is Christ, whose people saints, whose king the God of Love."
"Your talk is foolishness, poor man ! Think you we can be moved--
By frenzy such as this, you do but your own weakness prove."
"I say not of myself these words. I beg you take this book ;
It hath withstood both fire and sword. Now open it, and look
And for thyself read its true words. You see the fearful flood
Of sin and anguish that must whelm, unless saved by the blood."
"Tut ! with your book away, I say, will you with us return,
Or will you, like a senseless one, the voice of wisdom spurn ?"
"My hand unto the plow I've put ; within my heart doth burn
Such strong desire for that bright land, I would not now return
If all the world was offered me. Oh friends, I beg you heed
The warning of my book! 'Tis true. And while we run we'll read
Of that dread day when God shall come in vengeance dark and dire
To strike the guilty ones to doom and purge the world with fire.
Too late 'twill be amid the wreck to count the bitter cost ;

Your only cry in that dread hour will be, ' I'm lost! I'm lost!'"
"Of this dread future which you speak, I have no fears at all;
Your talk is like the silly words when babbling children call.
Come, Neighbor Pliable, let's leave him to his weakish way,
He'll see his folly and turn back before the set of day."
Said Pliable with smirkish smile: "I've listened all the while;
If what he says be honest truth, you sin, thus to revile.
It strikes me as I think on it I will with Christian go,
For to the judgment of that book I would not come, you know."
"What! go with him? Why, you will be the by-word of the town;
Be wise, be wise, Friend Pliable; make not yourself a clown."
"Oh friends, give heed!" poor Christian cried, "the words I've said
        are true;
This judgment is for all the world as well as me and you;
Escape we must, the book doth say, through Christ the only way,
Since in the blood alone is life, accept it I you pray!"
"You go your way, Friend Obstinate. To this I've made my mind,
With Christian to associate. These joys, I too would find."
"You'll get befogged, Friend Pliable. 'Twas only Christian's scare
That made him leave our goodly town, and on this venture dare."
"Not so," said Christian very bold. "I know whereof I speak,
Evangelist marked out the way. I'll find what now I seek.
We'll to our journey now, sweet friend;" and Pliable arose,
And bade "good bye" to Obstinate. With Christian then did close,
While Obstinate, with air of one who scorns and pities, too
Bade them—the poor misguided ones, a hasty, sharp adieu.
"I'm very glad I came with you, good Christian," with a smile
Said Pliable, in honeyed voice, "we can the way beguile
In talking o'er the gains we'll get from going in this way,
The riches, honor, peace and good, what are they, tell me pray?"
"Oh, words are very weakness, friend, when used to paint these things,
The human heart cannot conceive the joys this journey brings.
But, list me while I read my book, and then you'll catch a view,
Of glories that shine 'round about Jerusalem the New.
The great White Throne, the gates of gold, with gems bestudded rare,
Of crystal stream, with fadeless trees that heavenly fruitage bear."
"'Tis very beautiful, and I'm glad I choose to come with you,"
Said Pliable, as they strained on, "but are you sure 'tis true?"
Then Christian spoke in earnest words, "He shall its truth soon prove.
All this was writ for us by Him whose very name is Love,
And we shall crowns of glory wear; to us shall harps be given.
In glistening garments we shall stand and sing the songs of heaven.

II

No more shall death his icy hand lay on our fleeting breath,
For Christ has triumphed over all, and conquered even death.
The elders, too, and harpers more than thousand thousands, sing
Loud anthems to the Holy One, of heaven and earth the King."
"This is too good," said Pliable, " My heart vibrates with joy ;
But do you really think, my friend, these things will us employ ?
" Here in my book the Lord himself these things recorded hath
For all who will deny themselves, and tread the narrow path.
Most freely will He give to those who willingly receive,
Oh, hear him speak these loving words : ' Look unto me and live.' "
" You charm me much, good Christian friend. And now I surely know
That all you've said is very truth. Let's onward faster go."
Poor Christian sighed as Pliable urged him to quickened pace.
" This burden is a weight to me, I falter in the race."
" Come on, come, quick ! I would be there," in words so sweet and fond
Spoke Pliable. A few steps more, they reached the Slough Despond.
Both tumbled in. Both struggled fierce, but struggling. deeper sank.
About them was the slimy pit, above them vapors dank.
" Ah, me, we ne'er through this shall get," said he of foot so fleet ;
" If ever I from out shall come, I'll beat a quick retreat.
Where are you now ? You told me false ! is this the goodly land ?
Where is your 'record,' where's your crown, your harp ? in deathless
    hand.
Farewell, farewell, I turn about, and seek the certain good,
And leave you with your burden sore to tread the unknown road."
He gave a lunge, a dash, a leap, and gained the nearer shore.
Poor Christian seeking, burden-pressed, caught sight — then saw no
    more.
" I must get through, I dare not look back o'er the road I've come.
The wicket-gate, the wicket-gate ! and then I'm safe at home ! "
But oh, 'twas fierce ; despair came down and seized his very soul.
" I will believe, I'll n'er go back, but press on to the goal ! "
Help held her heavenly hand to him. He grasped it with a kiss.
She raised him up, and said, " Look there, the Gate you cannot miss."
" Look here," said Christian reverently, " I would a question ask :
Why in the King's highway this bog ? " " Ah, heavy be the task
That will repair this low descent where slum of sin doth run !
The King's choice men have labored hard, and still the work's undone,
Full sixteen hundred years they've toiled with patient, earnest zest :
It still remains a 'nasty slough ' for Pilgrims. And the best
That they have done is through its mire to place these heavy stones,
And every Pilgrim, though he sink, comes out with solid bones."

✦ TRIALS. ✦

The quagmire passed, with joyous steps he hastened o'er the plain.
His heart beat fast, his hope rose high: the end he soon would gain.
Here up stept one with pleasing mien, and words of sweet entice:
" You're journeying to the wicket-gate? Have you looked at the price
That it may cost you thus to tread this narrow, lonely road?
And then it seems, my friend, you bear a heavy, useless load."
" I'm told," said Christian, stopping short, " that if I reach that gate,
I'll leave this burden. Thus I haste; I would not be too late."
" And have you wife and children fond, and will you leave them all,
And all alone, of doubts and fears to bear the heavy thrall?"
" I have both wife and children fond, but in them find no peace.
This burden galls me to the quick, from it I seek release."
" You're mad, poor one. I beg you list to counsel sound and good.
Ten thousands of the sons of men have followed it, and stood
As giants, in the strength it gave. Have plucked a rose each morn,
And never yet amid my flowers have found a prick or thorn.
But tell me," said the sly old World, " who was the stupid bore
That told you to discard your load you o'er this way must go."
" He was a fair and comely one, benignant was his mien,
Evangelist he called himself. He was from heaven I ween."
" Hath quite a noted character," said World with marked leer,
If you will follow his advice you'll find it cost you dear.
You've bravely tried a mile or two and were besmirched with mud.
You stand in sorry plight, and more, your trial 's in the bud,
For let me tell you there await you hunger, sword and death.
I tell you true, and did I speak with my last ebbing breath,
I must this testimony plain, this counsel of a friend,
Place 'fore your judgment, that you know what sure must be your end."
With thoughtful face poor Christian stood while World his gloze
　　spread fair.
At length he spoke. His timid words to World's strong contrast bear :
" This burden is to me more grief, than all you have me told,
Relieved of this let what will, come. It's this that makes me bold."
" But let me ask you, halpless one, how came you by this load?
'Twas well enough your head to turn and cheat you in the road."
" I read this book, most honored sir, and then my burden came.
There must be one who will it lift. Oh, can you tell his name?"
" Pshaw, silly one! you're like to those who to high things aspire,

The weaklings who, discarding peace, are rent by strong desire,
And fain would pry into the depths of all things they may hear;
Instead of joy and happiness, they fill their cup with fear."
" I will not measure words with you, my burden is too great;
I must press on as best I can until I reach the gate,
And there I'm sure relief I'll find, and so I bid good day,
And hasten forward to my rest."
     " Heigho, my friend, I say,"
Called out old World, " Are you so blind, and far beside yourself,
As to give heed to Evangelist's words, the doting, silly elf.
Here, sit beside me, while I tell of one whose skill will cure.
My counsel, wise and friendly aid, I'm sure you'll never rue.
Now listen Old World's advice: There lives a most judicious man
  Called by most men Legality.
He lives in a small village, only a short distance, called Morality;
And he has the skill to help men off, with burdens like thine;
To him thou must go, he'll give relief. 'Tis the way I got rid of mine.
He'll be glad to see you, but if he is not at home, Civility, his son,
Can do as well as his father. Many can testify to what he's done, .
And if thou dost desire it, I will send for thy children and wife.
Houses are cheap, society fine, and you can lead a peaceful life."
CHRISTIAN. I am in a great dilemma, but if this counsel be true,
It is the wisest course to take thy advice, and thy road pursue;
Which is the way to this wise man's house? Will you please tell?"
WORLD. "Do you see that high hill?"
     CHRISTIAN. "Yes, very well."
WORLD. "The first house you see is his."

  * * * * * *

     Then Christian did as he said.
But when he reached it, the top laid over until he was afraid
That it would fall on him. His burden was heavier, did much tire
Him, and he knew not what to do, for out of the hill came flashes of fire.
Then he regretted how he had acted. He saw Evangelist drawing near.
Now Christian blushed with shame. Evangelist looked angry, and fear
Caused Christian to tremble. He asked, " Didst thou not flee from sin?
Art thou not the man I found?" But he was speechless before him.
" I see plainly I've sinned."
    EVANG. " Did you by my advice abide?
You are now far out of the way, why so quickly turned aside?"

"I met a gentleman who said I could go to the village which lies
before me,
And be relieved of my burden, have my family, and from all cares
be free."
EVANG. "What was he?"
CHRIS. "He looked like a gentleman, and at last
Prevailed upon me to yield, but when I came here couldn't get past
This hill."
EVANG. "What did he say?"
CHRIS. "Told me if I'ould believe
Him, that he would direct me how to get rid of my burden, and receive
Many pleasures, and that house-rent and provisions were very cheap.
He would send for my family, and we could the best society keep."
EVANG. "Now list to the word of God, see what you refuse,
Not him that speaketh, for if they escaped not, who did misuse
Him who spake on earth, much more shall we not escape if we turn
Away from Him, who speaketh from Heaven, and His commandments
spurn.
Thou hast thyself alone to censure, and now thou hast so soon begun
To reject the creed of God, and thine own thread of salvation hast
thou spun."
Then Christian fell down, crying, "I am undone, woe is me!"
Evangelist raised him up and said "All manner of sin, shall be for-
given thee."
Then Christian stood trembling, and began slowly to revive.
Evangelist said, "Give heed to me, it is remarkable that thou art alive.
The man who deluded thee, was Mr. World Wise Man, of this world.
He goes himself, and sends others to the town of Morality, and has
hurled
Many a soul into perdition. His devotion and church is Morality.
Because it suits men of carnal-minds, and a dreadful fatality
Has followed the advice of these moral whisperers, for it is to the cross
A sinner must look. Christ's blood alone must wash away the dross,
And let the pure gold shine. To be saved, you must on Christ rely;
Whenever you try to find an easy way, then your soul begins to die.
The Lord says, try to enter in at the strait gate, for strait is the gate
That leadeth to life, and few there be who find it; you must hate
Yourself for being influenced by this man, and for turning out of the way.
You must abhor his trying to make the cross odious, and perhaps
You may
Escape the wrath of God; the King of Glory hath thus spoken unto thee,
He that shall save his life must lose it, you must forsake all for me.

And Mr. Legality is the son of a bond woman, and can he set you free ?
Mr. Civility, his son, is a hypocrite, and like other men, cannot help thee.
Now let this lesson be deeply inculcated upon the tablet of thy mind,
That no smiles or persuasions beguile thee, take and bind
It around thy heart, and when thou wouldst depart from the true path
Of God to follow man's advice, it will sting thee, and thou wilt evade
   the wrath
Of an angry God." Then Evangelist called for a confirmation of what
   he had said.
Then came words and fire out of the mountain, and Christian felt as
   one dead ;
The voice, in awful tones, said, " It is written, cursed shall be every one
That continueth not in all things that are written and have not done
Them." Now Christian looked for death, and with a lamentable cry
Exclaimed, " What shall I do ? Is there no hope ? Must I in sin die ?
I truly repent that I e'er listened to that man. Oh, may
I expect forgiveness ? Can I now go to the gate ? I ne'er shall forget
   this day ! "
EVANG. "Thy sins are great, but God can forgive ; go in peace, and
   never
Listen more to man, lest God his love from thee sever."
Christian's heart oe'rflowed with gratitude, and he did lightly bound
O'er flower'd valleys, and ere he was aware, he found
A beautiful arbor prepared for rest ; here he went to sleep,
Like many do in prosperity, when they should their vigils keep.
When he awoke, to his dismay, he found it very late ;
So he hurried on. Two frightened men said, " Ah, the fate
That will meet you ! Two great lions are directly in the way."
CHRISTIAN. "What can I do ? I cannot return ; I must not stay
Here. Lost my roll, and all these difficulties meet
Because of my indolence. Now my torn and bleeding feet '
Must wander in darkness. Oh, I hear the awful roar
Of those lions ! I do repent ! I can never reach that shore
Of eternal peace ! But this is my way, I must not fear,
Even if death awaits me. What is that I see as I draw near ?
Two lions indeed ; but both are chained—now I will call
Unto the Porter, Alas, I'm too late ! This doth indeed appall
Memor e than the lions. Ah ! I hear an answer—'tis my voice,
Only echoed back to me. He answers. Now I will rejoice."

PORTER "Why so late my friend?"

CHRISTIAN. "I have a sin
To acknowledge: I slept too long in the arbor. Do let me in!"
PORTER. "Come into our palace prepared for the transient rest
Of pilgrims. Bathe thy bruised feet. Thou shalt have the best
We can prepare. Now we have here a great variety
Of curiosities. Let me introduce Piety and Charity.
Welcome, care-worn brother. We know something of thy trials;
But while journeying to the Celestial City we must meet denials
And temptations. But there are many things I would have you know,
And if you've rested sufficiently, I will them unto you show.
Do you remember, in the days of Pharaoh, when God
Told Moses to take His people from Egypt? This is his rod.
Here's the hammer and nail with which Jael slew Sisera; and then
The ox-goad wherewhith Shamgar slew six hundred men.
And the jaw-bone with which Samson did such mighty feats;
And the sword with which the Lord will kill sinful men when He meets
Them in the day of vengeance." And other things which did much
        delight
Him. Then they ate supper and retired, for it was late at night.
In the morning Christian felt much refreshed, and said, "I must go."
They told him to stay another day, and they would to him show
The Delectable Mountains, provided it was sufficiently clear:
:"And this will add much to your comfort, they are near
The Celestial City." So he consented. When the lovely morning came
They carried him to the observatory, and said, "Now look. The name
Signifies the loveliness of them." He looked, and saw mountain peaks
Towering over wooded glens and flowered vales.

CHRIS. "Ah! weeks
I could spend in wondering! Those fruits and fair flowers
Diversified o'er those grassy plains—the fountains and fairy bowers:
Tell me, is not this country called Immanuel's Holy Land?"
PIETY. "Yes; and free for pilgrims, as this palace. There is a band
Of shepherds who will the gate of this city show to thee."
"This makes me anxious to go on."

PIETY. "You must wait and be
Clad with the armor of God. These weapons will enable you
To get through."

CHRIS. "Have any pilgrims passed?"

PORTER. "A few
Have recently; I noticed Faithful not long since passed by."
CHRIS. I regret so much that I did not go sooner. Why

Am I behind others in zeal ?"

PIETY. "We'll all go to the foot of the hill,
With thee." As they went they told him not to despond, but still
Think of what he had seen, and that he must not be cast down.
Those who travel this road must see trouble ere they wear the crown.
When they reached the bottom of the hill his companions said,
"We must part. Here is a cluster of raisins, some wine and bread."

*   *   *   *   *   *

Christian knew he was in the valley of Humiliation, and many did yield
To a hideous fiend whom he saw coming near him, through the field.
Then Christian was afraid, and knew not whether to stand or run ;
He knew he had armor only for his breast, and if he tried to shun
His darts, he could not turn his back. Apollyon was terrible to behold,
Was covered with scales like a fish ; he was very vain and bold ;
Had wings like a dragon, and feet like a boar ; there came fire and smoke
Out of his lion-like mouth. He thus unto Christian spoke :
"From whence are you ?   What doing here ?   Whither going in such
    speed ?"
CHRIS. " I came from the city of Destruction, because I know I need
The help of God. I'm going to the city of Zion."

APOL. "I perceive
You are one of my subjects ; that city is mine. What shall you receive
For running away from your King ? I ought to with one blow
Smite thee to the ground."

CHRIS. " I was born in your city, I know
Your service is hard, your wages death. When I came to years
Of manhood, I saw the gulf over which I stood, and many fears
Came o'er me."

APOLLYON. "Since thou complainest, return and be content,
And you shall live in ease."

CHRIS. "Then I'll be rent
From the King of Princes. I cannot think of following another."
APOL. " Thou hast made a bad choice. I can easily smother
The contempt that some would feel, and the fears of thy breast
May annoy at first, but my advice will eventually give rest."
CHRIS. "Thou destroying Apollyon, I love my master's company,
His government, His country, better than thine. I'll never with thee
Live again."

APOL. " For His service, many have been put to death.
You say that His service is better than mine, and the last breath

Of His subjects was praise? Yet He never did deliver them,
But the world knows how by power, or fraud. In delivered men
Who followed me, I soon in their breast deep love awake,
No one can ever say they have been by me forsaken."
CHRIS. "God's refusing to help them, is only to try their love.
If they cleave not to him, they can ne'er dwell above.
Christ is an example of suffering, and the pain is glorious,
When their Master sends it, they will soon march victorious
When the Prince cometh with his host, and the trump sounds,
Then past tortures will be forgotten; the heart bounds
To meet its Saviour."

      APOL. "After sinning dost thou think
That thou wilt be in that throng? Thou art on the brink
Of eternal woe."

      CHRIS. "Wherein have I been unfaithful to him?"
APOL. "At the slough of Despond thou didst sin;
And you did not wait patiently to get rid of your load
Of sin, and slept and lost thy passport on the road.
Thou wast almost persuaded to return because 'twas night.
Did you not waver, and tremble, at the trifling sight
Of two lions? In all thy talk and ways thou art very vain,
And desirous of glory, which is evident to all: can thy Prince remain
Loving to thee, after thus acting?"

      CHRIS. "All you've said
Is too true, but for these offenses I trust that I have made
Acknowledgments. My Prince is merciful, and will forgive;
I was guilty of those sins in the country in which I did live;
I believe I have obtained pardon." And when he thus spoke,
Apollyon flew into a rage, saying, "I do now evoke
The lowest fiends of Hell to help me curse thy Prince; I hate
His laws, and Him, no one shall serve Him. Ah! the fate!
I will withstand. That now awaits thee; I will withstand
Thee."

      CHRIS. "Apollyon, Beware! I'm on my King's land."
APOL. "I do not fear; prepare to die! I do now swear
By my infernal den, thou shalt not go! I say forbear
Thy attempt, or thou shalt lose thy life; return; if you start
To go, you know your fate."

      CHRIS. "I must."

      APOL. "This dart
Shall pierce thy heart's core."

      CHRIS. "Do you see this shield?

It will enable me to withstand thee; I can never yield."
Apollyon then sent them with such powerful strength
That Christian, notwithstanding his exertions, at length
Was wounded in the head, hand and foot, which made him give way,
And Apollyon followed, and thus it lasted for half a day.
Christian was weak, and in making a desperate struggle, did fall.
His sword fell out of his hand. Apollyon said, " Now call
On thy Prince to help thee. Does he come ? Ah, dark despair
Is written on thy countenance. Lo man ! now, where
Is thy King ! This shall be thy last blow, 'twill crush thee."
Christian now struggled desperately, got his sword, and said, " Oh,
    enemy,
Rejoice not against me. I'm fallen, but will soon rise again.
Take thy deadly blow ! Ah ! this doth fill thee with terror and pain.
Thou art stunned ! You see we are more than conquerors through
Him." Then Apollyon spread his dragon wings, and away he flew.
When Christian was recovered, he saw the fiend no more,
But for hours after, the hills reverberated with his terrible roar.
Christian exclaimed, " Oh, Lord ! let me give thanks unto Thee,
My Deliverer, I know that in all danger thou wilt help me."
Christian sang : " Great Beelzebub, the Captain of this fiend,
Armed him, and thought he would ruin me. For this end
He sent him well prepared. None can e'er know his rage
Until they see him. Oh, how fiercely he did me engage.
When I had almost despaired, Michael came and helped me, and I
By dint of sword and one desperate effort made him fly.
Would that all could unite with me in singing praise
And love, and would bless my great Deliverer always."

    *   *   *   *   *   *

Now I saw in my dream that his wounds made him feel
Very weak. Then came a hand with leaves which did heal
As soon as they were applied. Then he ate the bread and drank
    the wine,
Which Piety had given him. He said, " Oh, the Love of God
    'tis Divine."
After being refreshed, he went on his journey with a drawn sword,
For he anticipated other dangers, but there was none on the road.
Yet there was a trial awaiting him, but God with His grace
Could support him in the Valley of Death, 'twas a lonely place.
Jeremiah thus describes it : A land where nothing dwelt;

A land of deserts and pits. And who knoweth how poor Christian felt
When he had to go all alone through this place. And what did he
See? One running toward him saying, "Go back."

CHRIS. "Tell me
Why I must turn back."

MAN. "There's danger; do you know the name
Of this dark valley?"

CHRIS. "Yes; tell me all."

MEN. "We came
To the border, and fortunately we there did meet."—
CHRIS. "What have you seen?"

MEN. "Take a seat,
And we will tell you all. The valley is darker than night;
There are satyrs, visions, dragons, pits, and directly in sight
Of this valley are the clouds of Confusion, there's the yell
Of a people in utterable misery. The worst we have to tell
Is that Death's wings are ever spread o'er this dark path."
CHRIS. "This must be my only way to Heaven. If God's wrath
Is poured upon me I'll pray, and will never be forsaken."
MEN. "You will be sure to repent of the steps you've taken."

*　　　*　　　*　　　*　　　*　　　*

Then Christian went with his sword drawn; could scarcely find
His way, 'twas so narrow. On his right hand was where the blind
Had often led the blind into a ditch, where both were lost;
On the left was a dangerous quag, which to many had cost
Tears, and even lives. Into this quag King David once did fall,
And would have perished, had not God heard his call.
Here many are lost. Ah! Virtue, exert thyself, and throw
Thy mantle around the world; shield them so they'll ne'er know
Of such wickedness. With Christian we'll now go again.
He found it difficult from temptations ever to abstain.
The way he had to go was narrow. He saw the flame arise
From the gaping mouth of hell. It made him close his eyes.
He sheathed his sword, and knelt in prayer for help. Ah! dire
Were the tossing and groans, which came with flames of fire,
To welcome him to this vale; then he met a mysterious shape,
If shape it might be called; he knew he could not escape,
For others came, and then a band of howling fiends was heard
Marching in front, their breath was poisonous, and the bird
That tolls the sick man's passport from her hollow beak,

In the silent night doth their sad fate often speak.
Her shrill notes chill, and she shakes contagion from her wings ;
She haunts this dismal place, and in darkness ever sings
Her doleful tune. All of this did greet Christian's ear ;
The fiends still came nearer. He said, " I will not fear
Them ; I'll trust in God and walk in His strength, I'll rejoice
In my trials." Then they left him ; he shouted, his voice
Rang loud and long. He anticipated evil, and he heard one say :
" Though I walk through the valley of the shadow of death, I may
Still hope, for in all my trials God will strengthen me."
This cheered Christian ; he knew that there were others he did not see,
And that God had blessed them ; he tried to overtake
Them so he could have company, but soon day did break,
And he exclaimed : " He who has traveled this vale may say
It is dark." He looked back at the dragons, and as the day
Dawned, he shed tears of gratitude when, by the light,
He could see the dreadful pit, and loathsome quag which, in the night,
He had passed. The glorious sun came to brighten the day ;
He could see what he had to contend, with the rest of the way.
Dungeons, pits, and quags, and many other things did show
Themselves, frightful to behold, but he said others did go
Through the same dangers. There were two giants, and not a ray
Of mercy shone o'er their palaces, and the bones of many lay
Around their dwellings. But their race was run ; God above
Had heard His saint's cry, had seen their anguish, and in love
Had crippled them. Their names were Pope and Pagan. By
Their tyranny they had reaped the reward of sin ere they had to die.
After Christian had passed them he said, " Oh, I'm blest,
To thus escape their snares, they cause a blight, and no rest.
I'm delivered from Hell, with all its darkness and sin ;
I knew not of the many dangers which were in
That lonely vale ; they might have cast me down
If it had not been for my God, and may the crown
Ever rest on His brow."

     *   *   *   *   *   *

Now he saw Faithful : as he went
On his way he never loitered for vale or ascent.
Christian hurried on and called saying, " I will go with you."
FAITHFUL. " The avenger is behind I must pursue

My journey." Then he ran faster, and tried to overtake
Faithful—he would have a companion that would ne'er forsake
The true path of duty. This made Christian admire him more.
He kew that was the right way, for he had done so ;
When those wicked men tried to persuade him to return,
He refused to listen, and their idle rumors did spurn.
Christian came up with Faithful and said, "I have met
With a congenial spirit. How long since you started ? I can ne'er
    forget
Those loved ones which I've left. Tell me all. How long did you stay
In the city of Destruction ?"

          FAITH. My heart ached and I tore away
From those I loved. Some said the city would be burnt to the ground.
CHRIS. "Did many leave ?"

          FAITH. "They did not, and I found
Much skepticism. I heard some of them deridingly speak
Of your pilgrimage. I believe 'tis a doomed place and I do seek,
A land where there will be no tears to dim my eyes—
A home where Seraphs dwell, and praises of saints arise."
CHRIS. Did you hear of Pliable ?

          FAITH. "We heard you
And him journeyed together until you came to that slough,
Where some said he fell in. I believe it is the decision
Of most of the town, he is held in great derision."
CHRIS. "Why are they so bitter ? They will not come in the way
Which he forsook."

          FAITH. "They call him Turn-coat, and say
He is not worthy to stay with, because he has forsaken
The true path."

          CHRIS. "Are you not mistaken ?"
FAITHFUL. "No. I met him in the street, and he tried to shun
Me ; he is, evidently, much ashamed of what he has done.
Hence the proverb, 'The sow that was washed has returned to her
    mire.'
Many are thus deluded and perish. Let's leave him, for I tire
Even of his name."

          CHRIS. "Tell me of your journey."
FAITH. I escaped the Slough of Despond, which I see you fell
Into, and without any trouble I soon went
To the gate ; but after I passed, there was a demon sent,
In the form of a woman. She was beautiful, and paraded all
Around me. I knew her smiles had caused many to fall,

Yet, I lingered, enchanted by her charms ; then up the rugged hill
I climbed ; there came one swiftly by, then I stood still.
His looks indicated vengeance, and with a powerful blow
He brought me to the ground. I cried ' Mercy !' He said, to show
Mercy on one who could not resist temptation, and then again
The blows came. Ah ! I hope that I'll ne'er feel the pain
That he inflicted. I know not how long it would have lasted ' Forbear'
Was heard. I saw His hand and side, I knew my Lord was there."

CHRIS. " The man who overtook you was Moses. He spareth none,
Neither knoweth he how to pity those who willingly shun
His law."

FAITH. " I know him, oft he has met with me.
'Twas him that warned me of my danger, and caused me to flee
From God's wrath."

CHRIS. " Did you not see on the side
Of the hill a house with lovely grounds ? "

FAITH. " Yes ; the Guide,
Or Porter was there. The lions were asleep ; 'twas about noon.
I thought I could not lose so much time ; 'twas too soon
To stop for the night."

CHRIS. " I'm sorry indeed ; the rarity
Of all I saw would have paid you, then I would have had your
       company
Where I've been so lonely. Whom did you see in the valley
Of Humility ? "

FAITH. " Discontent. I strived and did rally
My feelings to such a height, that I could easily resist him,
Though he said I would offend my friends—' Pride ' puffed with sin,
' Egotism,' ' Mr. Worldly Glory,' and others ; and I was foolish enough
       to wade
Through this lowly valley."

CHRIS. " What arguments were made ? "
FAITH. " I told him those persons were not related
To me, and never would be. I would ever resist him ; I stated
Plainly that honor was preceded by humility, and that a fall
Followed a haughty spirit, and that I did not wish men to call
Me wise."

CHRIS. " Did you meet any other person here ? "
FAITH. " I met one who had neither principle or fear,
And I think of all men bears the most inappropriate name.
Why 'twas given is a mystery, it is Bold-faced Shame."

CHRIS. " Why, what did he say ? "

FAITH. " That religion was to him
Something very degrading, a tender conscience a great sin.
It was effeminate to watch your ways, both night and day,
And to restrain all evil passions, and try in every thing to obey
The mandates of the so-called book of God, and they did not possess
Any quality of a man. That religion did not relieve any distress,
And that most pilgrims were humble, and few of the world's wise-
Men were on this dishonorable road; that it did surprise
Him to see me. He said that there was no pleasure to live
Thus struggling with the turbulent ways of sin; and to forgive
One's fault, or to ask pardon for your own, was to him
The most ridiculous of all things. 'Twas only a childish whim."
CHRIS. " What did you say ? "
FAITH. " I could not tell
What to say at first; his words sounded like those of Hell.
I told him what is highly esteemed among men, is held in abomination
With God—that he was only a sham. Men of every station
Were discussed, but he knew nothing of what God's Word is,
Or its commands. At the judgment day, what will his
Arguments avail him ? We will not be judged by the world,
But according to the law of God, we will either be hurled
Into everlasting peace or woe, and what God says is best
That the world with its allurements might go, if I was blest.
I told him of the Power of Christ, and man a serpent when he hates.
Our Redeemer, I would follow him though the Fates
Combined should exert their energies ever against me.
Then I told him to depart, that I would no longer keep company
With one who only showed the dark side of religion. In vain
Were his efforts to tempt me. I told him that I did him disdain."

*　　　*　　　*　　　*　　　*　　　*

Then they noticed a man who soon overtook them, and had much talk :
FAITH. " Wither art thou going ? for thou dost walk
Very fast. If you are journeying to the heavenly country, let me
Accompany thee."
TALKATIVE " I'm on that road, and 'twill be
A great source of pleasure for us to hold concourse of things,
Which send their radiance o'er congenial spirits, and brings
The future as if it were within our grasp. But few

Care about profitable conversation. I am glad to meet you."
FAITH. "'Tis to be regretted. I think the tongue can ne'er fill
So high an office as when it speaks of God's good will
Towards men."
TALK. "I agree with you. If a man has any delight,
'Tis when he can discern in another the same love. The sight
Is like the reflection of a mirror. What a halo of love divine
Doth o'er shadow two pure minds when their thoughts and words
combine,
But our very thoughts are evil, and we can do nothing of ourselves, or
receive
Anything, unless 'tis given us; all is of grace I sincerely believe,
And for this confirmation I could many Scriptures bring."
FAITH. "We must come to something definite. One thing
We must select, and base our conversation."
TALK. "Anything you will
Select suits me, heavenly or earthly, up or down the hill
Of adversity or pleasure, any current in which you row your boat,
So it will be profitable, in it I will cheerfully float."

*　　*　　*　　*　　*　　*

Then Faithful was amazed, and stepping to Christian, said:
"We have a brave companion—a noble pilgrim he has made."
CHRIS. "This man has deceived you. His fair speech and smile
Will allure you; from the right path he can beguile
All who listen to him."
FAITH. "Ah, do you know him, then?"
CHRIS. "Yes, better than he knows himself, and most men
Regard him as a foul hypocrite; his name is Talkative.
I'm astonished you do not know him, he dwells near where you live
In the same town."
FAITH. "Whose son, and on what street doth he dwell?"
CHRIS. "He lives on 'Flattery Row,' and is the son of Say Well."
FAITH. "I may know him; he has the appearance of a gentleman."
CHRIS. "He has indeed, but he assumes much; when abroad he can
Easily deceive; at home he is known better; most things look best
At a distance."
FAITH. "I'm inclined to think you jest."
CHRIS. "I may have smiled, but God forbid that I should
Accuse any falsely. He would talk very fluently if you would
Present any subject whatever. He is very wise; no frown

Of yours can teach him you are tired, and he will be down
On your principles when from you."
                             FAITH. " From this hour
I will remember the Kingdom of God is not in word, but power."
CHRIS. " I've noticed him closely, and even the dumb brute
In his kind serves God better. Yet he has the audacity to refute
The opinions of any ; he is a disgrace to religion, and a shame
To any community ; he is ill to his family. But it is vain
To try to enumerate his faults. Not satisfied with his sin, he makes
His sons follow in his footsteps ; he detests all that's good ; the rakes
Of the town abhor him."
                            FAITH. " I'm astonished, but you say
That you know him ; I must believe, though 'tis very sad, and from
        to-day
I will try to penetrate deeper into every man's thought
Before I form an opinion so hastily. I would have been caught
By the fascinating language of this man, had not you led me
Into the secret of his character. Now I can plainly see,
Much can be assumed by sinful men, and as David says,
' Often their words are smoother than butter, yet they have for days
Been drawn swords.' Too many of this class we now meet,
Who seem to worship you, yet their hearts are full of deceit."
CHRIS. " If I had not known him, I would have thought as you did ;
Or, if I had obtained it from any other source, would have hid
It within my bosom, thinking perchance some enemy
Was trying to injure him. What I've said is true, and thus you see
Him clothed in the garb of deception."
                           FAITH. " This does instill,
More deeply than ever, that talking is not doing God's will."
CHRIS. " 'Tis diverse indeed, the boaster's soul is often dead,
And such egotism is offensive ; for often what is said
Sinks like evil seed, sends forth plants of sin ; but pure
Religion is to keep yourself unspotted from the world ; 'tis sure
To visit the widows and orphans in their affliction. But *that man*
Never thinks of the practical part of religion—thinks he can
Reach Heaven by his tongue. Hearing is naught—save some of the seed
It requires watching and praying, to keep rooted out every evil weed.
Men will be judged according to their works ; at the day of doom,
The secret thoughts of every heart will be known. Ah ! the gloom
Which will o'ershadow many a countenance. The end of the world
Is compared to our harvest, and Alas ! how many will be hurled
Into perdition."

FAITH. " Paul says, talkers are ever giving sound
Without life—like sounding brass, and men of this kind will be found
In every country—though they have an angel's voice, raise the lid
Of the outward character and look within."

FAITH. " How can I get rid
Of him ? "

CHRIS. " Enter upon some discourse of the power
Of religion. Ask him about his pleasure in it, and in half an hour
He will tire of you."

*　　　*　　　*　　　*　　　*　　　*

FAITH. " Ho, Talkative! What cheer now ? "
TALK. " Thanks, I'm well. Thought we should have talked more. How
Is it you've been absent so long ? "

FAITH. " Christian and I
Commenced an interesting conversation, and so the time did fly
More rapidly than I was aware of. I did not think I staid so long,
But we will commence our discourse."

TALK. " A song
Before would be pleasant."

FAITH. " How doth the grace
Of God manifest itself in the heart ? Often in the face
Is a true index into one's character. Opinions plainly show
The channel of one's thoughts, and by their conversation we can know
On what ground to place them."

TALK. " This great outcry
Against sin, when there is grace in the heart, we will now pass by
This theme, hurriedly."

FAITH. " No grace makes us abhor sin."

TALK. " What is the difference of crying against and being in
Utter hatred of it ? "

FAITH. " You can condemn through policy,
But you cannot abhor it, but by virtue of antipathy
Against it. I've heard men abuse it in the pulpit who did abide
It well enough in the heart—remember Joseph's mistress cried
With a loud voice, pretending she was very innocent and chaste ;
Notwithstanding her guilt and deception—List to her cry, ' Help!
Haste ! '
What wickedness ! Her breath more poisonous than a reptile's fang,
For they can reach only a short distance, but her hideous voice rang
The death-knell to poor Joseph's hopes ! Ah! sure the poor man knew

His fate—Yet he feared God.   What a lesson!   Ah! how few
Would have acted thus!   He is more to be commended than Azim,
For the affection of a fair Zelica taught him to resist sin,
But Joseph, un exiled servant, to resist the entreaties of a majestic
    queen,
Knowing, too, he would excite the wrath of the king.   Yet, how serene
Is innocence!   No paleness, or blush came upon his placid face
When he heard the verdict: 'Cast him in the dungeon!' for the grace
Of God he knew would shine e'en there; His ways are not as ours.
    The cloud
Of adversity o'ershadowed him, and in gloom's dark shroud
He was covered; yet he despaired not, but said, 'I will ever trust
In God, though He slay me.'   When he was into the dungeon thrust,
There was one light which cheered him, even in this dark
And lonely cell; Hope found her way, and send her spark
To comfort him.   How God blessed his future every child doth know;
But few follow his example, which doth so plainly show
That if we wait patiently, the Lord will certainly bless;
And when He afflicts sorely, 'tis not because He loves us less
But to return.   A mother often cries out in anguish against her child,
But soon forgets, and begins to cherish her darling when it is mild."
TALK. "You are inclined to misconstrue, I perceive."
                                       FAITH. "No, I
Am only for having things right.   What's the second thing whereby
You'll prove the discovery of the work of grace in the heart of man ?
TALK. "Great knowledge of gospel mysteries, but my first plan
Was rejected, I expect this will be too."
                           FAITH. "This should
Have been first, for you know, knowledge never could
Be obtained 'thout grace.   I tell you, a man may possess
Unlimited knowledge, and be a child of Satan nevertheless.
Do you remember Christ asked, 'Do you know all these things?'
And He said, 'Blessed are ye, if ye do them.'   And this brings
Many similar passages to my mind.   Give me knowledge, and I
Will keep Thy law.   I will observe it with my heart."
                             TALK. "You lie
At the catch again—this is not for edification.   Will you propound
Any question, or produce any argument, whereby grace may be found
In the heart of man?"
                TALK. "I cannot give any."
                            FAITH. "May
I mention some ? "

TALK. "Proceed!"

FAITH. "It showeth itself in this way;
It presents to our view our sins, and brings to us deep conviction,
And shows to us plainly, unless we curb our passions, and place
    restriction
Upon our habits, we will be lost, and this causes sorrow for sin
We find a revealed, a forgiving Saviour, and see the need of worshiping
    Him,
Then we can plainly see, it is to us so many promises are made
And according to our strength of faith, our joy will increase or fade.
Though it manifests itself thus, yet we very seldom conclude
That it is a work of grace. On a contrite spirit doubts oft obtrude.
To some it is discovered by a confession of faith, and a holy life
Answers to their confession, not one of contention and strife
With our neighbors—in this way acts the hypocrite, for in
All his ways he rejects God. The Christian always abhors sin.
I have given you my opinion of grace, in as brief
A manner as possible; object if it does not meet with thy belief;
If not, I wish to ask another question."

TALK. "It is not my part
To object. I will enter upon any topic with all my heart."
FAITH. "Do you experience the first description, and
Doth your life testify to the same? or do you now stand
Condemned before me? Be careful, I wish you to say no more
Than God will approve, and your conscience justify. You know,
He who commendeth himself is not approved, but whom God doth
    commend.
It is a sin to say you are a Christian, when acts with words don't blend."
At this Talkative blushed, but when his control he did recover,
Replied: "You now come to experience and to God, and I discover
That you appeal to Him for justification; all you have spoken
Has taxed my patience. I did not anticipate this: 'tis not a token
Of a pleasant companion. I am wounded and will not answer. You
    chastise
Without any ground; the whole tenor of conversation doth surprise
Me much. Explain why you have thus acted."

FAITH. "It is because I saw
That you were very forward to talk, and that perchance a flaw
Was in your life. Without farther equivocation, I have heard of you
    before;
Your religion lies chiefly in your talking, your boasting and your show.
True religion fares the worse for you. Your sins cause some to stumble

Into the ditch of deceit, into which you are now ready to tumble.
The proverb is true of you, as of a harlot: even your very name
Is a reproach to Christians, just as the harlot is to woman, a shame."
TALK. " Since you are so hasty in your opinions, I know you
Are some inconsistent person. We do not suit, so I bid you now adieu."

* * * * * *

Then Christian came up and said : " Did not I tell you how it would be ?
He had rather leave your company than to reform or to agree
With your sentiments. Let him alone : he is only a boast and a show.
We are happier without him, and he might have disgraced us ; you know
The apostles say : ' From such withdraw thyself.' "
          FAITH. " I am glad
I had this discourse with him, when he reflects it may make him sad.
He was angry when he left. I talked very plainly to him ;
My conscience is clear, if he is immerged in the gulf of sin."
CHRISTIAN. " I think you did right in talking to him as you did ;
Generally we are too careful of feelings, and often much is hid
From the eyes of the church by a cloak of wealth. They fear to offend
An influential member, when their actions ne'er did blend
With those of a true Christian. This looks strange to the world, I
    believe
If all such were rejected, the church would be stronger, and receive
More members. They would be more careful how they tampered with
    this theme,
Ah! how sad to think foul men often use it for their scheme ;
By which they cover their darkest sins. Talkative raiseth his plumes,
How confidently he speaks, and what divine language he assumes,
To deceive and baffle all ; but only behold him as soon
As Faithful talks of heart-work, he reminds us of the moon
Which is past the full, it begins to decrease and into the wane it goes,
And so will all who follow him, for Talkative never knows,
Aught save his foolish prating about what he has seen by the way."
CHRIS. " He thinks only of himself. God's commands he does not obey.
Brother, your company has been a great pleasure to me, and many
    lonely hour
Has been banished by your sunny smiles. Ah! how great the power
Which true friendship hath. But oh! degenerate men, how few
Are there in whom we can confide. Their flattery wins you,

But oft like a serpent they coil around your heart, and instil there
Their deadly poison. 'Tis sad to think so, but we had best beware
Of most men and women."
FAITH. "Misplaced confidence is why
So many suffer. Oh! who comes yonder? who is it we doth espy?"
CHRIS. "It is our good friend Evangelist. 'Twas he who set me in the
    way.
To the gate." By this time Evangelist came up, and unto them did say:

     *   *   *   *   *   *

"Peace be unto you, dearly beloved, how is it with you? Doth the night
Of darkness still continue?"
CHRIS. AND FAITH. "Ah! the sight
Of you banishes many dark forebodings. Our troubles and trials
We will relate. But when we asked God for mercy, we ne'er met with
    denials.
His strong arm has brought us safe thus far."
EVANG. "I'm glad
You have resisted so many temptations; the trials which make you sad,
Will eventually benefit you. I have sown and you two have reaped.
But the time is not far distant when blessings will be heaped
Upon both the sower and the reaper; persevere, and you will be made
Heirs of eternal life, be crowned with glory that never can fade.
Remember, only by faithfulness these blessings you can obtain.
Oh! that the whole world would arouse and drop the curtain over
    the vain
Trifles of life. Then we would not be allured by fascinating sin,
But would look into our selfish hearts, and by God's help search in
Their lowest depths. Then God will give unto us strength and power
To resist the Evil One, for he cometh in an unknown hour."
Then they both thanked him for his advice, and desired him to speak
More about their journey; how to resist trials, and how to seek
The glory of God.
EVANG. "It is through tribulation that the grace
Of His kingdom is entered into. You will be afflicted, and each face
Will be ploughed by the furrows of sorrow. You will soon see
A town, where some will seek to murder you; an enemy
Will be met, in the guise of a friend; yet, the King will give
A crown of glory to the faithful, and then you can live

Through eternity. But in this life you must suffer much pain,
Yet you will be strengthened by thoughts of future joys. And again,
I say, do not be discouraged ; God will help. When you have come
To the town, quit yourselves like men, and let the bright home
Where the blessed Redeemer and shining angels wait for you,—
Let this encourage in all trials, and help to resist them. Ah! the view
Of your celestial home! Now you see, you are almost there.
I must tell you of a Fair, kept there, which is called " Vanity Fair."
It is as old as injurious ; I will tell you something about it, and when
It did originate, almost five thousand years ago, and then,
·Beelzebub, Apollyon, with all their foul companions perceiving
By the Pilgrims' path, they had to go in this way, and receiving
Many enticements, they might be led astray—for all kinds of games
Are constantly played there. Various are the streets, but their names
Are too numerous to mention. Pilgrims are compelled to go through
    this town.
They must go out of the world, if they do not pass through this city of
    renown.
The Prince of Princes, while here, went through this wretched place,
And Beelzebub, the chief Lord of the town, with his brazen face,
Offered our Saviour all the kingdoms of the world, and thought
He would allure Him to buy, but his devices came to naught.
Beware! Farewell!'

    ✳   ✳   ✳   ✳   ✳   ✳

➤✱ VANITY FAIR. ✱←

THE pilgrims had to go through this 'Vanity Fair,'
And as soon as they had entered, behold! What a great
confusion there !
On account of their different clothes. This made the people gaze,
Yet they wondered much at their speech, which did much amaze
The whole town, for the pilgrims spoke the language of Canaan
but they
Who kept the Fair, were men of the world, and what they did say,
Seemed uncivilized and ridiculous. But look! How they try
To induce them to buy; but they would not. Their only cry
Was, "Turn away mine eyes from beholding Vanity," saying
their trade
Was in heaven. This caused the town to mock them, and soon made
Much confusion. Then they unto their chief did send,
To see if he could ascertain these men's business, and put an end
To their strange talk. Many questions were then asked of them.
They answered—"they were pilgrims, going to Jerusalem,
And had given no occasion for such talk or vile abuse ;
They had been asked to buy things for which they had no use."
They told the chief, his men knew that peace was wanted, yet they
Pretended not to believe them, and did indignantly say :
"You have created so much discord your punishment is severe ;
You must be beaten, and your fine garments we will besmear."
Then they beat, and put them in a cage—the ruler of the Fair still
Laughing as all his subjects did. Yet the men resisted not ill
For ill, but blessing and kindness, for injuries which were done.
Then there were men in the Fair, less prejudiced than some
Who were so enraged. They tried to check the wicked, and did blame
Them for beating the pilgrims. The excitement was great, and the name
Of confederates was given them, that they, too, should partake
Of the caged men's trials ; yet they were sincere, and would not forsake
The slandered men ; but their zeal increased the anger, and they
were beaten again ;
But they bore it without a murmur. Then they were ironed,
and a chain
Was fastened on each one, and they led through the town,

As an example and terror to others.   Yet they cared not, so God did
    not frown
This treatment Christian and Faithful with so much meekness bore,
That it won to them many men who were enemies, and, as before,
It created more disturbance.   Then it was very soon concluded
That neither irons nor whipping was sufficient for these deluded
Fanatics—nothing but death would satisfy their hate.
The pilgrims called to mind what Evangelist had said of their fate.
They comforted each other by saying, the one who suffered most
Would soonest reap eternal joys, and be with the blessed and the just
Then they commended themselves to God ; they knew He would fulfil
All righteousness, therefore they waited prayerfully until
Their judgment was passed.

      ✱   ✱   ✱   ✱   ✱   ✱

              When the time arrived, they were brought
Before their enemies and arraigned, and all the evidences sought.
The judge's name was Hategood.   Their indictment was one
And the same in substance.   The contents were, these two had come
As disturbers of the trade, and that they all plainly saw
These men's opinions were dangerous to their Great Prince's law.
Faithful said he was able to bear their sentence ; he had tried
To defend his Maker ; he was for peace, but their prince he defied,
Because he was Beelzebub, and an enemy to his Lord.
Then the proclamation for all who had one word
To say against the prisoners.   Then there came in three
Who were ready to accuse them.   Their names were, Envy,
Superstition, and Pickthank.   The judge said : " You'll now proceed."
       Then came forth
Envy, and said :   " I have known this man a long time, and can attest
    upon oath,
That he doeth all he can to entice men in his path and follow his ways
And notions, which he calls principles of faith.   I think, in these days
Of refinement, that they are absurd and ridiculous.   He says
       Christianity
Is diametricallly opposed to the customs of our town Vanity,
By which saying, my Lord, he doth not only condemn
All of our laudable acts, but also us in doing them.
I know much more, but do not wish to be tedious.   If you need
Me, I can testify to more.   I assure you he is a 'noxious weed."

Judge said it was sufficient. Then dark-hearted Superstition made
His appearance—Said: " I know little, yet I wish it would fade
Forever from my mind. He is vile, and makes our religion naught."
JUDGE. " This is enough, without any more evidence being sought."
But Mr. Pickthank had to come and tell all he knew against this
Prisoner. Said: " This man speaks of another home, and the bliss
Which he will enjoy, and on our noble Beelzebub ever rails ;
And speaks contemptuously of his friends, whom he never fails
To designate—as the Lord of Carnal Delight, Sir Greedy,
Lord Luxurious, Desire of Vain Glory, and the rest of our nobility ;
And he has not been afraid to abuse you, who have his fate
In your hands." When Pickthank finished, the judge said :
  " Thou runagate,
Heretic, traitor, hast thou heard what these men witness against you ?"
FAITHFUL. " May I speak a few words in my defense ? "
                            JUDGE. " Dost thou pursue
Thy course of audacity, in making such a request ? But speak,
That we may show how kind we are, ere we our vengeance wreak."
FAITH. " In answer to Envy I said, ' things which pleased his god were
Very much opposed to Christianity,' if this be amiss, I will bear
Any reproach. I cannot make any recantation. I only said
That in the worship of God, faith must fill the heart, and what is
    forbade
In His word, I rejected ; that I believed it was of divine revelation.
Therefore, what is thrust into the worship of God by any nation,
Which is not profitable to eternal life, will come to naught ; and for me
To explain what Mr. Pickthank said, is useless, for I plainly see
That the Prince and his subjects are combined, and are demons
    from hell,
Whose business it is to deceive all they can, and here they dwell,
Until they are repulsed by God's power."
                          Then the judge called
The jury who stood by, very much excited and appalled
At Faithful's bravery. " See, gentlemen," said the judge, " this man
About whom such an uproar has been made ; now you can
Hang him or save his life. Yet, I think it best to instruct and aid
You all I am able. In the days of Pharoah—servant to our Prince—
    he said :
' Those of a contrary religion had multiplied much and had grown
Too strong for him. He commanded the male children to be thrown
Into the river. And there was another act made in the days
Of Nebuchadnezzar, that if all did not follow in his ways,

And worship his golden image, they should be thrown
Into the lions' den. If he had broken a few laws, I could have borne
It much better. This is not only in thought, but in word and deed;
For he has openly defied our laws. This must be stopped. He
    doth need
Immediate punishment. Pharoah's law was in due time
To suppress anticipated trouble, but here is apparent crime.
He acknowledges he holds our religion in great contempt.
And for the vile treason he confesses, he cannot possibly be exempt."
The jury then went out to consult. Their names were, Mr. Nogood,
Blindman, Malice, Loveleast, and close by these,
Mr. Liveloose, Highmind, Enmity, and Mr. Hatelight,
Who unanimously voted against him, saying they had acted right,
For he was worthy of immediate death. Then they all in haste
    out went
Unto their judge, to talk of the most torturous way they could invent,
To put this foul traitor out of their sight. Faithful to his cell did retire,
Until he was sent for. List! What shouts! Look at yon fire!
How bright it burns, as though some sacrifice would be placed there.
But alas! The greatest of all sacrifices—a human form doth appear.
What means those knives, those stones and those swords? Ah! what
    terrible pain
They will soon inflict.

*   *   *   *   *   *

    But where is Faithful now ? Will he not again
Make the same daring avowals ? when he doth plainly see
How many ways of torture they have. Hear him speak. "Unto thee,
Oh, Lord ! I commend my spirit unto thee. Their swords, fire
    and stake
Can only punish me a while. I will never fear or quake,
Neither do I revoke what I have said. Inflict any punishment ; I
    can stand
It without a murmur, for I will be supported by my Saviour's hand."
And patiently he hears their mocking, as they predict his doom.
Not a word escapes his lips ; no dark shade of gloom
Covers his radiant face, but like brave Stephen of old,
He appeared like an angel. 'Twas faith that made him bold.
How many of us would have renounced religion ? Watch him how
    he dies.
His lips move in prayer, and to heaven he lifts his eyes.

And, lo! a chariot is seen behind yon burning cloud.
The sweet echo of angels' voices charms mine ear, but a shroud
Of gloom is o'er Christian. List! a trumpet spoke of his celestial fate.
What are terrestrial sorrows, if they are the nearest way to the gate
Which leads to eternal happiness? Then Christian no more weeps,
But cries: "God knoweth best. He searcheth into the deeps
Of the inmost heart." But now, Christian's journey we will trace,
And see the end. Back to prison he was sent, and he stayed for a space
Of several weeks. But his Father ordained his escape one day.
Then Christian went singing and rejoicing on his way.
He often thought of Faithful, and said: "Pure man! he did profess
His Lord openly and met death bravely, and God will surely bless
Him eternally, while faithless ones with all their delight
Are crying out for more blood, saying, 'tis their legal right
Thus to murder. Faithful, thy name through ages will survive;
Nations will ever call thee blessed, and though dead, art yet alive."

➤✳ NEW COMPANY. ✳◄

HEN I saw in my dream, that Christian went not alone,
For there was one, named Hopeful, who was ever prone
Travel that road, though he needed courage, and being at
    the Fair,
And seeing how Faithful died, it made him jealous, and just there
He resolved to follow in his footsteps; and he wished to go
With Christian, for he had much experience, and he well could show
Him many useful things. Faithful died to testify to the truth,
And another rises out of his ashes—even this hopeful youth.
He told Christian that many of his friends would certainly come;
That Faithful's death would surely cause others to seek the home
To which Faithful had gone. His example to many will teach
The true road to God. Look. They overtake one from Fairspeech,
Whose name is By-Ends, yet he seemed very loth to tell
It, after giving the name of his town. Christian asked, "Can any dwell
In this place and be innocent?" He answered, "I hope so." But
        his name
He evaded. When Christian asked it, he reddened with deep shame;
He feared Christian had heard of him; said, "I'm glad of your company,
If you are going in this direction; you are a stranger to me."
CHRISTIAN. "I have heard of this town. Fairspeech is a place
Of much wealth."

BY-ENDS. "It is indeed, and many a kindred face
Greets me when there."

CHRIS. "Brother, I hope you will not tire
Of my inquisitiveness, who are your relatives? I desire
To know them."

BY-ENDS. "Lord Turnabout, Timorous, Speechfair,
From whose ancestry the town took its name; and there
Are many others—Mr. Smoothman, Mr. Talking-Both-Ways,
Mr. Anything; and the pastor of our parish says there is praise
Awaiting our great nobility. He was my mother's only brother.
And if time would allow, I could tell of many other."
CHRIS. " Are you a married man?"

BY-ENDS. "Yes, I am, of course. My wife

Is a model—the daughter of Lady Feign—and my life
Is serene. Even in this religious storm, we never strive against tide,
But when everything glides smoothly on, then we love to hide
'Neath the sunny folds of Religion's cloak, and to sing
With others when loud applause of religion doth ring
Through every street."

        Then Christian stepped a little aside,
And said to Hopeful: "It runs in my mind, as he doth hide
So much, he must be the notorious By-Ends, and I tell you, if 'tis he,
We have a most villainous knave, as bad as bad can be."
HOPEFUL. "Ask him; he will certainly give you his true name."
CHRIS. "Sir, If I mistake not, sir, I have heard of you."
                BY-ENDS. "My fame
Has spread far."
        CHRIS. "You are egotistical, and By-Ends
Must be your name."

        BY-ENDS. "This is but a nickname, friends,
I scorn those who gave it me; but I must be content to bear
It as a reproach, as other good men before me, for you know there
Never was a worthy man unless the slime of slander was thrown
O'er him."
        CHRIS. "That's true. Your character is well known
Abroad; your neighbors say you merit it, or you would erase
The cause of so many rumors, bringing on your head disgrace."
BY-ENDS. "My attempt to do so has caused censure, some will load
Me with reproach."
        CHRIS. "Your conversation betrays you; this road
Cannot be traveled peaceably by both of us at the same time,
For I believe you deserve this name, and your thoughts and mine
Are altogether different."
        BY-ENDS. "You are rude, and you'll find
In me an agreeable companion."
        CHRIS. "You'll have to bind
Up these broken places in your religion, and against wind and tide
You must go, and ever own our religion, though in rags you must
    not hide
From Him when He is in irons."
        BY-ENDS. "You require too much. Leave
Me to my liberty; let me go with you. I cannot just believe
As you do about all things."
        CHRIS. "Not one step, unless you

Consent to follow my advice."

By-Ends. "That I will never do.
I can never desert my principles, for I know that there
Is no harm in them, and much profit. Therefore I shall prepare
To go alone, until I meet some one of a congenial mind."
Chris. "Farewell. You may plenty of company find."

*   *   *   *   *   *

And thus they separated. But Christian on looking back
Saw three men coming. And By-Ends his pace did slack,
And received them cordially, for their feelings did well blend
In one, and they were happy. Mr. Hold-the-world, and By-Ends
Had been to school together, to a Mr. Gripman, in Lovegain,
The county seat of Covetry, where dwelt Mr. Loveall. And in vain
Were the efforts of the spirit to remodel this place. Here the art
Of accumulating was taught, oft religion was assumed. The dart
Of evil had never been broken, but sin had sharpened it, and now
We see those specimens of wickedness, not caring how
They manage, so they make a show. Now, Money-love spoke,
Asking, " Who are those before ? Suppose we try to provoke
Them to stop."

By-Ends. " They are strange men, who after their mode
Are going on pilgrimage. Yet, they are so very rigid in their code
And manner of thinking, they shun others, and do lightly esteem
Their opinions. If you do not agree with them, they will teem
Many an insult upon you."

Loveall. "There are some of whom we read
Who are over-righteous. They condemn all. They say when the seed
Of repentance has never been sown in the depths of the heart."
Love. "Did you differ on many points, ere you did with them part ?"
By-Ends. " Yes. They firmly believe 'tis their and every one's duty
To press forward to the prize ; That religion has its beauty,
Even in rags and persecution. Even then, they say, we must cling
Tenaciously to it, and when the solemn bell doth doleful ring
Its deadly knell for execution, they like fanatics believe
That we ought to stand steadfast, and prayerfully receive
Any fate God seems best to inflict, and adhere to Him, although
The whole world should condemn them. They don't believe in show
Or display,—are humble, yet careful with whom they associate.
Yet, I know that I am better than they. Such arrogance I hate.
I like religion when he is basking in the pleasant sunshine

Of prosperity, but if there be any risk about me, or mine
Estate, then I forsake Him. For I believe in taking care
Of yourself."

Mr. HOLD-TO-THE-WORLD. "We all would fare
Badly if we did not look after worldly things; let us be wise
As serpents. How contemptible a poor man looks in the eyes
Of the world! I think it better to follow the example of the bee,
Which lieth still all winter. When the weather is pleasant you see
How busy it is. We know that God sometimes sends rain,
And then sunshine, and they act very silly. Abraham was not vain,
Yet grew rich in religion, Solomon, Job, and others, I intend to pursue
Their path."

LOVE THE WORLD. "I am sure I'll agree with you;
And we can enjoy this world and the next, and none of these
    troubles see,
And leave to these hapless, foolish wights their tears and misery.
He who rejects our theory has neither sense or scripture, and
    don't know
Anything of his own liberty. Such men never want any more
Knowledge."

BYENDS. "We are all satisfied, and from this dullard thing
Let us divert our minds, and more weighty questions bring
Before our thought. Suppose a minister is a tradesman,
And has a good chance to improve his fortune, and he can
Do so by not being so particular, even if he doth lean
To a few points of religion which he doth not admit, and can screen
Himself from censure."

LOVEALL. "I think like you, and can't see
How any one could object. With these friends' permission, I'll tell thee
What I think of it: First, take a minister, who is possessed
Of but little, many there are who are sorely and often distressed.
If such an one can manage, in a respectable way, to acquire
Wealth, there is no harm if he revokes his principles, and doth desire
Thus to accumulate a nice fortune, there's no impropriety
In thus acting, I think that he must be convinced that he
Is called from above. This is in accordance with the law,
For if providence has given the chance, I cannot see the flaw
In it. I think it makes him in every respect a zealous man,
And as for complying with the ideas of his friends, I can
See nothing improper in that, it shows he can himself deny;
That he has a fair deportment and a good supply
Of self-denial, which makes him more fit to fulfill

His ministerial duties, and the mandates of God's will.
And as to the second part of the question which we view,
Let us suppose a minister to be poor, and with a chance to pursue
An easy path to wealth, by taking a rich wife;
Men will soon forget it all. Then he can enjoy life.
If any one becomes a Christian, he needs not to forsake all, and then,
It often helps to improve one's fortune, and they are held by men,
As the best of the world."
                  This opinion of Mr. Moneylove made
A great impression on them. Applauding it much, they said :
" We cannot see how those conceited gentlemen can refute
What Mr. Moneylove hath said, should they with By-Ends dispute.
What do you think of it my friends ? Let's call to them again.
It may divest them of their vanity, and our trouble will not be vain."
" Agreed," they all cried ; " Now let Mr. Hold-the-world propound
The question ; and they cannot oppose him, for he is ever found
Ready to give them an answer."
                 They called—asked the questions. Then,
Christian said, " Even a babe in religion could answer them.
Your own language condemns you, for, if it is a great sin
To follow Christ for loaves, you should see the error you are in.
For if this be wicked, how much more so is it for you, to make
Of Him and religion instruments of enjoyment. You must forsake
The world. And there are none, save hypocrites, who thus believe
As you do. The heathen Hamor, and Shechem, when they wished
    to receive
The daughters and wealth of Israel, and saw there was no other way
For them to accomplish their desires, yielding to the law did say,
' We must be circumcised.' And you can read and plainly see
What they did by assuming a religious guise. The Pharisee
Is a good example of hypocrisy. A long prayer for his pretense
But to rob widows of their homes. God's anger was intense.
Judas, the traitor, was of this religion, he wished to better his
    condition
When he took the bag. You know that he was a son of perdition.
Simon the wizard was of this religion, for he would have had
The Holy Ghost in order to get money. But, alas ! what a sad,
But appropriate sentence Peter passed on him : He who doth take
Up religion for the world, will for the world forsake.
Judas betrayed his Master for the love of money ; now, therefore,
To answer the question affirmatively, as you have, and to show
That it is authentic : Your opinions are heathenish and hypocritical,

And your rewards according to your works, diametrical
To all that is pure."
            Then they all stood in wonder, gazing
At each other, thinking the courage and talk of Christian most
      amazing.
They were disappointed, and traveled in silence for miles ; and then
Christian said to Hopeful: "If they cannot withstand men,
What will they do when they shall hear the sentence of God ? If mute
When dealt with by vessels of clay, how can they hear the rebuke
Of an avenging God ?"

*   *   *   *   *   *   ·

            Then Christian and Hopeful left them again.
And very soon they came to the border of a beautiful plain.
Their enjoyment while crossing this was great ; yet it did not last long,
For soon they discovered a hill called Lucre, and then their song
Of pleasure ceased, for there was a silver mine in the cave,
Which had attracted many to woe, for there was naught could save
One who should reach the brink, for the ground would break,
And destroy immense numbers. The whole earth would shake
So, that some were terribly maimed, and not until the day
Of their death be themselves again. And this is the sad way
In which millions have been lost. Then I saw in my dream
One Demas. A man of courtesy, and he called, and unto us did seem
To have naught else to do, save to entice others. He cried, "Ho !
Turn aside hither ! I have something of great interest to show."
CHRISTIAN. "What is it that can deserve our attention more than
      the divine
Way of God ?"
            DEMAS "Here is where you can get rich, and a mine
Of pure silver is here. Many are digging, and if you will only come,
You can provide for your families, and then you can go home."
HOPEFUL. "Let us go and see."
            CHRIS. "Oh, no ! I've heard of this place,
And how many have been slain. It has caused numbers to turn
      their face
From the true God."   ·
            Then Christian called loudly unto Demas,

Aud said: "Is not this place dangerous? If I mistake not, it has
Been the ruin of thousands."

DEMAS. "Not very dangerous." Yet he blushed
As he spoke.

"Then," said Christian, "Let every word be hushed
About going to this place."

HOPE. "If By-Ends has as we
This cordial invitation, I know he will turn hither to see."

CHRIS. "No doubt, for his principles lead him in this way."

"But will you not come and see for yourself?" Demas continued to say.
Then Christian answered plainly: "Demas, thou art an enemy
To the right way of the Lord, and art condemned by His majesty.
And why seekest thou to bring us in like condemnation?
Because thou art cast off, do not envy others their salvation..
And if I turn aside unto thee, our King and Master will hear,
And will put us to shame, when we unto Him would near."
Then Demas said: "Wait awhile. I would like very much to walk
A short distance with you. There is a vast deal I would talk
To you about."

CHRIS. "Certainly. But first tell us your name."
"They call me Demas. I am the son of Abraham."

CHRIS. "The same
As I thought. Gehazi was your great-grandfather, and you
Are son of Judas Iscariot: as they did, so you do.
And this is only a fiendish prank of yours. You know your father
     was hung
For a traitor, and you deserve the same fate, for you have often rung
The death-knell of many a pilgrim by your smooth words,
Which David says are oily like butter, but yet they are drawn swords."
By this time Mr. By-Ends and his companions came in sight.
They went to Demas immediately. Ah! the terrible plight
They soon were in! How wretched they felt when they in terror found,
How they were deceived. "Beware, oh, beware, for this is dangerous
     ground!"
Thus sang Christian. And By-Ends and Demas doth quickly agree,
One calls—the other thoughtlessly runs, that he, too, may be
Undone by the gloze of Mammon's snare, and thus you see how
     these two
Take up in this world together, and their dreadful path pursue.

* * * * * *

Now I saw on the other side of the plain, that they came
To a place where an old woman stood, but there was no name
Written on this statue, which at firs' they could see. Thoughtfully
    they stand
For a long time, but after examining closely, in a mysterious hand
Was written something that troubled much—they found it to be,
" Remember Lot's wife!" Ah! this is a warning for all to see,
And think of the covetous desire that caused this woman to look
Disobediently. Ah! Brother, this fate must surely be told in your
    book.
Every sinful pleasure that glides by we must ever shun;
Oh, let us ever this lesson remember, lest we, too, be undone.
Then Hopeful said somewhat to himself, "I acted like a fool.
There's difference slight between me and Lot's wife, for I would have
    been a tool
For Demas, if you had not interfered. For only looking back, she
Was made an example. Lo, I have done worse. I longed to go and see.
Let Mercy plead, and may I ever hang my drooping head in shame
That such wickedness should be found in my heart. Ah! the fame
Of this mine of silver: how many a pilgrim it hath already beguiled.
For Demas' tongue is smooth as oil. I was ready to run when he
    smiled."
Then Christian spoke gravely, as he looked at his friend : "Of that we
    see here,
Let us take notice for admonition in the future. It doth appear
That the woman had escaped the destruction of Sodom, and then fell
By her sinful desire ; and as example is standing here to tell
All to beware of covetousness."
                   HOPEFUL. " We should shun her sin,
For there was Korah, Dathan and Abiram, and two hundred and fifty
    who in
Their wickedness perished. These say, ' beware !' But now, above all,
I wonder that Demas with his train do not into misery fall.
They pipe and they play, they dance and they sing, while here,
This pillar stands as a lesson to all of them, and yet they have no fear,
And will not listen to warning."
                 CHRIS. " How desperate they have grown !
In the same way the recklessness of rogues in the presence of judges
    is shown.
The character of these thieves is in every respect, like these men
Of Sodom and Gomorrah. What sinners they were ! A— then,
It is said, they were sinners before the Lord, and did stand

In His presence, and sin, notwithstanding the fruitful land
Was compared to Eden, with all its beauties, and therefore,
This made their plague greater, and provoked God's anger the more.
And so it is with these people, they have eyes, but do not see;
Ears, but cannot hear, and God's judgments surely must be
Severe to the last."

HOPE. " What a miracle we are alive !
We can never cease to praise our God—not only spared, but thrive
Well on our journey."

     *   *   *   *   *   *

While they talk a river comes in sight,
Which is called by David "The river of God," and with untold delight,
They discovered that their way led to this crystal stream,
And now beneath its cooling shades the wearied travelers dream
Of that Celestial City where God will forever smile ;
Where grief and tears are aye unknown. Here resting awhile,
They then awake. Calm and refreshed they are: scarcely can believe
That it was real. The trees were clothed with graceful leaves
Which, when applied, healed all diseases which did about abound.
The earth was filled with indescribable beauty, and the ground
Was covered with lilies, which filled the air with perfume.
Here they rested several days before they did resume
Their journey. Then they sang, "How the crystal streams soft glide,
For the joy of foot-sore pilgrims, down every mountain side,
A great variety of fruit and useful leaves these trees do ever yield,
If every one could see, they would sell all and buy this field."
They rejoiced with grand acclaim ere their journey they renewed,
And being much refreshed, their onward path pursued.
But now they leave the stream, and find the hither way
Is very rough indeed, yet they dared not stop nor stay,
And as the hours passed by, the weary pilgrim's feet
Were very tender grown. They would a better way seek, when lo !
    they gladly meet,
A path leading into a meadow. Then said Christian : " Now if this
Cool meadow's in our way, it cannot be amiss
That into it we turn."

HOPEFUL. " But if it leads us out of the way ? "
CHRIS. " That is not probable, for it goeth by this road, and we may
Travel much easier here."

→✳ CASTLE OF DOUBT. ÷ GIANT DESPAIR. ✳←

AND now they see a man walking before,
Whose name was Vain Confidence. They call to him to know
Which way that pathway led. He answered,
"To the Celestial Gate."
Then they followed, but night came on, and lo! the dreadful fate
Which seemed them to await. T'was dark, and they heard the fall
Of Vain Confidence in some pit; then both did loudly call—
No answer to them came, only the echoes of his terrible groaning.
Christian said, "I am to blame, and I can never cease my mourning,
For this my great sin, in turning aside." Then rain began to fall,
And Hopeful said in tears, "Henceforth, I'll keep my way, nor on a
    stranger call.
It's vain for man to plan."
                    CHRIS. "Do not be offended
With me; I was sure that we were right. I never intended
To bring evil on us."
                    HOPE. "No, Brother, you have misunderstood
Me; I did not wish to censure you, I believe this will be for our
    good."
CHRIS. "Let us go back as quick as possible, I will go
Before, so if there danger be, 'twill come to me."
                    HOPE. "Oh! no,
Your troubled mind may lead you wrong again."
                    Then there was a voice
Heard for their encouragement. This made their hearts rejoice,
For it directed them to turn hastily back toward the plain highway,—
·"And when you see by-paths, do not, dare not, in them stray."
And now the waters rise—they both were filled with pain,
And with all their perseverance they could not reach again
The stile, but finally came to one, where hopelessly they fell
Asleep. Here Giant Despair found them, and who can tell
Or imagine their dismay, for he dwelt in a castle of Doubt.
He grasped them with a clutch, and in anger loud did shout
Unto them to be up—his prisoners, they must go
With him to Doubting Castle. Ah! this filled them with woe.

Then he forced them on before him, and in a dungeon dark,
Reeking with filth, most noisome, where they lay without a spark
Of fire or glimmer of light. The Giant told his wife, at last
He had two prisoners, and wished her advice. He told her he had cast
Them into the deep dungeon. Then Diffidence, his wife, said: "Beat
Them unmercifully." And this he did, from their head to their feet,
So they were unable to move. Then left them to condole
Over their suffering dread. Their weeping and sighs were heard, but
    none came to console.
The Giant's wife then said: "Indeed you must advise
The prisoners to kill themselves." He came with his glaring eyes,
And harsh voice, telling them to put themselves to death. "There is
    a fine supply
Of poison near you both. 'Tis a most pleasant way to die."
He carried them to the castle ground to show them the skulls, to fill
    them with sorrow;
And said: "You had better destroy yourselves. You know not what
    to-morrow
Will bring forth." Told them how he had saints torn to pieces. And
    as the dawn
Of day came on, he took them out. Ah! the contrast of that morn,
And the dark prison in which they had dwelt for days. He let them
    to behold
The bones of those whom he had slain, then said: "As you were
    pilgrims bold,
This your fate must be, 'fore ten days run their round,
Unless you kill yourselves." Then drove them under ground.
The Giant and his wife consult again. She said: "Perhaps they may
Intend to escape." The Giant answered: "I do not know, but by the
    break of day
I will make all things sure."

                   But now we must return
To Hopeful and Christian. They lay in blood, and the fever seemed
    to burn
Their very vitals, fierce. Lean starvation seemed to stare them in
    the eyes,
With all the Giant's threats. But Christian cried with surprise:
"Oh! Brother, how foolish I am! I can walk at liberty!
Why have I forgot that I have in my bosom a key,
With which to unlock Doubting Castle! No longer now be sad.
We will spend no more days in this dungeon dark. Come hither up
    and glad

That we shall soon be free !"   He took his key and tried :
The old door opened wide.
Then joyously they ran unto the castle yard, and behold a door
Was there.   This was unexpected, but their key opened this also.
They knew that one more gate must to them opened be, ere they could
      pursue
Their journey, and with one desperate effort they thrust it open too,
But it made such a noise it caused the Giant to awake,
And he asked,   " Who is there ? "   But one of his spasms did shake
His awful limbs, so he could not walk.   And thus we often see
That much can be done by faith and with fair Promise's key.
With elastic steps they onward go, until they reach the stile
Where they erred.   But they were thinking all the while
Upon some plan, to warn others of this terrible Giant of Despair.
They concluded it would be best to erect a pillar there,
On which was written, " Over this stile is Doubting Castle, so beware !
'Tis kept by one who seeks to destroy pilgrims—even Giant Despair."
After arranging this, they went on their way rejoicing, and sang :
" There are thorns concealed 'neath every rose, each sin doth bear a
      fang,
Which is more poisonous than the venom of our rankest reptile.
We must travel God's road, though it brings a tear instead of a smile.
We have learned by sad experience, for out of the way we went, and found
What it was to follow our own device, and tread forbidden ground.
Let all who follow us, reflect, and certainly beware
Of this place, lest they for transgressing, Old Giant's prisoners are."

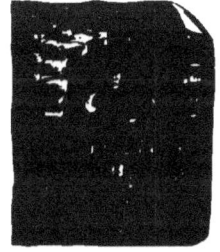

→✳ DELECTABLE MOUNTAIN. ✳←

THEN they went on rejoicing, until they came to the noted
mountains,
Which belong to the Lord of the Hill. There they beheld
the fountains
Of crystal water, and the rays of the sun made it appear
As though a holy light o'ershadowed them; and they now had
naught to fear.
The waters sparkled, and Zephyrus with his perfumed wings
Hovers o'er this fairy ground. "But hark! Who is it sings
With that melodious voice? Ah! then another, and now the whole
Choir join. Were such notes ever heard? These strains dissolve
my soul
In ecstacies, and bring all heaven before mine eyes; this is a dim
Reflection of brighter joys. Who would not try to cleanse his heart
from sin,
To taste of heavenly bliss? Look at the fair guardians, which tell
Of our King's love to weary pilgrims—By sin we fell
Into the Giant's hands, or we would have been happy."
Now a voice
Echoes o'er the mountains. (They knew it was a shepherd.) It made
their hearts rejoice.
After reaching him they asked—"Whose mountains, and whose
sheep?"
SHEP. "These are Immanuel's mounts, and we His shepherds keep
His land and sheep. The latter He laid down His life to save."
CHRIS. "Is this the way?"
SHEP. "Yes, you are right."
CHRIS. "Is the road safe?"
Then he did say:
"It is safe for whom it is prepared, but transgressors shall fall
Therein."
CHRIS. "Is there any relief for pilgrims?"
Then he did call
Another one, who said, "Our King directed us to entertain
Strangers; therefore, the best of the place is before you."

And as the rain
After a long drouth, refreshes everything, so did this cheering news,
For they had not recovered from the Giant's stripes.   And now the
            ·dews
Of the eve bade them retire ; but when the shepherds found
That they were wayfaring men, many questions they did propound,
And being pleased with their replies, a hearty welcome gave
To the Delectable Mountains. " Soon your home you'll reach, you
            have but to be brave ;
'Tis over there."
        Then the shepherds, whose names were, Watchful and Sincere,
Knoweldge, and Experience, said unto them, " We wish you to
            stay here
Awhile, and get acquainted with us."
                            HOPE. " With pleasure we will stay,
For we feel that we can learn so much to help us on the way."
And being fatigued they retire, and sweetly do they sleep,
In this fair, rosy bower, by nature built,—for angels ever keep
Their faithful watch o'er pilgrims here.   And not till the king of day
Brightened the lovely, rosy morn with his golden, glittering ray,
Did the weary pilgrims shake off the drowsy mantle of slumber,
And rise to see the wondrous things about them, without number.

        *   *   *   *   *   *

The first was a mountain, Error called, which was very, very steep.
They bid them look adown its side.   They saw men, whom they keep
For an example. After seeing all the wonders new, they then desired
            to go,
But the shepherds said, " We must to you the beauteous City show."
They took them to a grand mountain ; the shepherds called it " Clear,"
And gave them their perspective glass, and asked what did appear.
They tried to see, but as they strove, before their vision came
The horrid sight they just had seen, which unexplained remained.
And yet they thought they something saw, much like the golden gate,
And glimpses of City Beautiful, sweet foretaste of the fate
Of those who hold out to the end, and on they went, glad, singing.
" How thankful," each to other said, " that every day is bringing
Something to encourage our souls ! By these shepherds, secrets are
            revealed

To weary pilgrims, which from others are strictly kept concealed.
Let every one to these shepherds come, if they would plainly see
Things miraculous and hidden, which to others, mysteries be."
Then the shepherd gave each one a note to guide him on his way.
One bade them of the flatterer heed; another to them did say,
"Take heed, and see you do not sleep on the Enchanted Ground."
And the fourth bade them God-speed!

*   *   *   *   *   *

I awoke, and lo! I found
It but a dream.   But then, lo! I slept, and lo! I dreamed again
Many things I will tell you, which I hope will not be in vain.

➜✴ THE COUNTRY OF CONCEIT. ✴⬅

SAW the same two pilgrims haste over the glorious mountains,
Whose lofty peaks were crowned with snow: from them
gushed glad fountains.
Below these mountains, lies the country called Conceit, and on the left
hand
There was a crooked lane entering into the road, and here did stand,
A polite lad named Ignorance. He bowed gracefully, and Christian
asked him,
Where he was from and wither going?
IGNOR. "I was born in
A country to the left of here, and going to the Celestial City you see.
CHRIS. "How will you get in?"
"As other good people," said he.
CHRIS. "At the gate you may be disappointed, what have you to
show?"
IGNOR. "I can tell. I am a good liver, pay what I owe, and I know
My Lord's will. I pray, fast, pay tithes, and have left now
My country."
CHRIS. "Thou dids't not come in the right way, and how
Canst thou expect to be received? I fear the name of thief
And robber will be given thee, at the last day. Thy belief
Is as much entangled, as the crooked lane through which you've come.
IGNOR. "You are strange to me. I heed you not, I'll reach my home.
I'll go my course, you can go yours. I'm sure all will be well
With me, and none from our country goeth now by the far gate you tell
Me of. We wish not this way to know; we have a lively green
And shady lane, which meets the way, and many in it are seen
To travel cheerily, but few go by the little gate."
Now, when they saw the man
Was wise in his own conceits, they said unto him: "A fool can
Have more hope than you, for a fool walketh by the way,
And when his wisdom faileth him, willingly doth say,
'I am ignorant.'"
CHRIS. "I think it best we have no more conversation with him,
And have him to reflect a while. I tell you this egotistical sin

Is possessed by many. It is best to give him time to muse
On all we have said; and sure I hope he'll not refuse
To take our advice. I feel sorry, he is young, and must remain
In the greatest darkness about things of the greatest gain."
HOPE. "I think it is best not to talk to him. Let us pass
Him by, and talk when he comes up again, for the mass
Of his kind cannot bear reproving. They always appear
So perfect in their own eyes, that they cannot bear to hear,
Or read anything contrary to their thoughts. They don't believe they
    are clay
Moulded by their Creator. But how different in that day
When judgment comes! What will they have to cover then their
    guilt ?
Money causes many to be silent, who ought to thrust to the hilt
Their swords of contempt, into the deceptive trunks which we see,
Sending forth branches of envy and lust, until the full grown tree
Becomes like the upas. Ignorance always thinks none has a thought
Superior to his own."

      *   *   *   *   *   *

      Now while they talked, Christian caught
A glimpse of some one coming down a very dismal lane.
It was a man possessed of seven demons, and, oh! the fearful pain
Depicted on his countenance! Christian said 'twas Tyranny,
For all knew that he was a knave, and dwelt in the town of Apostasy.
But Hopeful noticed more closely, and said on his back was written
"Wanton Professor," and "Damnable apostate." Now they both were
    smitten
With horror, at the number of demons, and the way he was bound.
But after they passed, they recovered from their fear, when they found
They were alone again. Christian said: "This calleth to my mind
An incident recorded of a man, who could ever bind
But little faith to his weak heart. He lived in the town of Sincere.
His name was Littlefaith. On entering this passage here,
There comes a lane, by Broadway, it goes by the name
Of "Deadman's Lane." Many murders have been committed at
    the same,
A place which is not far from us. Here Littlefaith fell asleep,
And there happened along three dirty rogues, who stealthily did keep

A daily watch for travelers, Guilt, Faintheart, Mistrust; three
Noted for infamy, and deeds of darkest dye. Look here, we see
Littlefaith just awaking. They all commanded him still to stand;
At this he became frightened, and nerveless grew his hand,
His comely face was white with fear; they took him at great odds,
    and Mistrust
Ran to him in a frightful manner, and immediately thrust
His spear into his side, and thought him dead, as prone he lay;
Then the thieves thought they heard some one, and said, " We may
Yet be taken, let us go, there is that man Great Grace,
Who dwells in the city of Good Confidence. Let us now retrace
Our footsteps quickly." They thought they had left Littlefaith to die,
But he recovered, and mightily cried for mercy. And when help
    came, how shy
He was of his old enemies! He was much afflicted and distressed by
His sad loss—his jewels he dare not spend, but oft did cry
With hunger."
HOPE. " His pass he would not yield, by which he would receive
Admittance at the Celestial gate. Ah! verily I do believe
I should have parted quickly with most anything, before
I would have suffered as he did—his sorrow none can know."
CHRIS. " Ah! he acted wrong, but nothing could have made him sin
So greatly, for he never could have been admitted in
The celestial city—rather would he have met all the thieves
Than to have been refused at the celestial gate; there he receives
Eternal joys."
HOPE. " How unlike Esau, who sold his birthright
For a mess of pottage; 'twas his greatest jewel, and his might.
Not so Littlefaith, he would not sell his jewels. How many this dark
    path pursue!"
CHRIS. " I acknowledge that Esau sold his, and so do
Many others, but you must some difference put, I ween,
'Twixt Esau and Littlefaith. How contrary their estates! Just lift
    the screen
From off thine eyes. Esau's birthright was only typical,
But Littlefaith's jewels not. Though he was in a strait most critical,
He was not tempted with desire to give up his treasures, and he
Would not willingly fulfill the lust of the flesh, but you see
That Esau did, for he said, ' I am now at death's very point,
Forsooth; what good will birthright do me now ? I'll anoint
My head, be merry, satisfy my appetite.' But not so with the man,
Even of Littlefaith, for you see, soon after acting wrong, he began

To show that his faith made him able to act aright, and resist all
Such vile temptations; Esau had no faith, not even a small
Proportion, and do you marvel that when the flesh bears sway,
That any one will sell his birthright: yea, will even pay
All that he has; but Littlefaith could not, and here is your mistake."
HOPE. "I acknowledge it, and your severe rebuke will make
Me more careful, though my ire 'gainst you was stirred."
CHRIS. "Im glad you've wisely heard.
A true friend holds the mirror square lest others darkly see,
And forget the words of this my book, and fail from wrath to flee.
But to our subject let us look. The thieves were scared and ran away.
If Littlefaith had shown any courage, I dare say,
He would have gotten rid of these cowards without loss. Why
Did he not attempt to defend himself? and if necessary fly?
Or yield when there was no other remedy? I really think,
If he had displayed any courage, he would have made them sink
Into utter nothingness.
                    HOPE. "Yes, some do think this way. I've read
Of many who talk bravely, but when come the days of trial,
They are like those who admire religion in wealth, but make a denial
Of it in adversity, and as for a great heart, Littlefaith none had.
Alas, your idea of attempting to fight and run, how very, very sad
To thus express yourself! And should they soon appear
Before you, would you not, like poor Littlefaith, be filled with fear?
You must most careful be, examine wisely too, considering again
That they are but journeyman thieves, and their efforts must
          prove vain,
If you are prepared for them. These wretches serve the king
Of the bottomless pit, and he will quickly spring
Up to their aid. His cry doth cause all to tremble. It doth sound
Like the roaring of a lion, it shakes the solid ground.
I too have been engaged as was Littlefaith, and 'deed
It was a struggle fierce. I tried to overcome, but when they were
          in need,
Their Master to them came. I was duly clothed in armor of
          fire-proof,
And though I thus had shield, it was hard to keep them aloof,
For they are very vigilant, and conflict stand; but they
Could not withstand Great Grace, and had his orders to obey."
CHRIS. "Yes, they have often fled, and their hideous Master too,
But they are brave; only be prepared, and my advice pursue.
You must remember Great Grace is the champion of our King.

Where Littlefaith would bring disgrace, he would great glory bring.
And this recalls the difference between two other men
Whose deeds stand out in contrast strange, writ by the eternal pen.
David combatting with the King, overcoming by God's help. Some
    are weak,
And others strong. The latter must bear with the former, and seek
Consolation for them. I would have done this, had I been Great
    Grace."
CHRIS. "Yes, but he would have had a struggle. Look you at his face,
Then you can find the deep-marked scar, which tells of the great trial
Which he often undergoes. When we think of Davids' faith and
    then of the denial
Made by poor Peter, who was thought to be the pride of all
The apostles, even a weak maid causing him to call
Out for fear and trembling to deny his Lord. The thieves give call.
Their king comes on, assisting in the fight. And never soul
Had armor more bedight. The breath of their king is as foul gas,
More poisonous than the reptile; 'tis dangerous to pass
Near him, for fire and brimstone come out of each nostril;
But if a man had Job's horse, and had the skill
To manage him, he might do many wonderful things,
For his neck is clothed with thunder, and he always brings
Terror and astonishment; with impatience he paweth the valley,
And in his strength he goeth forth when men in war doth rally;
He swalloweth the ground with fierceness, and the roar
Of the battle with its fearful carnage, doth not frighten more
Than the pleasant music of his own fair happy land.
But such footmen as we, I doubt whether we could stand;
Therefore, we ought not to desire to meet them, or, when we hear
Of others' weakness, boast ourselves—such are apt to fear.
Think of Peter—whom I've mentioned before—his foolish mind,
    and vain,
Made him to say he would do things he had not strength to do. Again,
When we hear these robberies are done, we should go prepared,
With shield and helmet, burnished well, remembering how one fared
For leaving his defense behind when Leviathan would not yield.
Therefore, He who knows hath said, 'Above all things, take thy shield
Of faith, wherewith ye shall be able to ward off the darts
Of the Wicked One,' who ever waits to pierce unwary hearts.
This shield of faith caused David to rejoice when he was in
The Valley of Death; and Moses preferred death rather than to sin
And be without his Lord. My Brother, if He will only go

With us, we have no cause to fear. He will comfort us, I know ;
I've engaged them once, have no desire to do so again ; I fear
That we are not out of danger. It may be they are near.
But I was not destroyed by the lions—I hope God will e'er deliver
Me from all dangers. What would we be without this glorious Giver
Of every good ? Now Littlefaith had been among the thieves,
Was robbed, came near getting killed, and whosoever believes,
Should be instructed, so you may more than victors be
Over ten thousand foes, and Faith will shield and strengthen thee,
E'en in the darkest hours of gloom."
                    And as they talked they went
On quickly. Ignorance followed hard, for yet he was sore intent
On overtaking the travelers. Just here they see a road
Leading into the one they walked. Its presence did forebode
Perplexity, and maybe grief, for neither one could know
Which one to take. But one called out and said that he would show
Them the right way. that he was bound to go to the same place.
They followed him, but soon they saw also the stranger's face
Was turned in an opposite direction, and before they were aware,
He led them into a net. They lay pleading with him to spare
Their lives ; they were much entangled, and could not extricate
Themselves. Then Christian said : " We might have escaped this fate,
If we had strict attention paid to what the shepherds bid.
They told us to beware of such talk as this one did :
These who spread nets for others' feet. They also gave a note
About the journey, and if we had remembered David, to quote
What he has said concerning the work of men : he said, I've kept
From the path of the destroyer, by the words of Thy lips.' " They
        ne'er slept
Any during the night. Lo ! a shining one came—a whip in his hand,
And he asked them whence they came ; and when he did stand,
Looking very sorrowful upon them, for they told him
Of the man who had deceived them, and had made them sin,
So he rent the net, and let the men out ; then—" Follow me," he said,
" That I may set you in your way. Come." And then he led
Them back to the path, and asked them then, " Where did you stay
Night before the last ? If with the shepherds, you have a note of
        the way."
They said, " Yes. "

        MAN. " Why did you not read, when you came to a stand ? "
Said they, " We forgot."

        *   *   *   *   *   *

Then I saw in my dream, he had cords in his hand.
He told them as many as he loved he rebuked, and they must lie
Down, and he chastised them there. He told them they had their
    supply,
And they could go on their way, and ever after to take heed
To what the shepherd had told them, when they did need
Any direction. Then they went singing, and were glad to get clear
Of their trouble so easy. Still, they were filled with fear,
For they had been deceived by one who wilfully beguiled.
But those who appear the fairest, are often most defiled.
Then they sang, "Come listen! you who walk along this way,
Learn something from our example, do not go astray,
If you are ever caught you will be put in a strange net,
From which you cannot safe come out, if you should e'er forget
The directions given you. We are rescued, yet you see,
That we are severely scourged, so let us your warning be."

    ✸   ✸   ✸   ✸   ✸   ✸

While singing thus, they espied one on foot hastening from the gate
Which led to the Celestial City. He asked them if their fate
Depended on their journeying. They said God did compel
Them to go on or to be lost. Their trials they could tell,
Of sufferings, too, and ups and downs, yet thankful for it all.
At this Atheist commenced to laugh, and told them of the fall
They sure must meet, for it was true they never would receive,
Them at the gate. Said Christian: "Do you think, poor one, that we
    believe,
One word of what you say?
                 ATHEIST. "There is not a place
Like the one you speak of, and the sooner the better you efface
All such foolish ideas. When I was at my home,
I heard of this great city: have sought it, but have come
To this conclusion, that it is absurd to think of it, and I can refute
Any argument you can bring forth."
                 CHRIS. " Have no time to dispute
With one so firmly set in wrong; say, Brother, can this be true?
He has traveled farther than we."
                 HOPE. "Is it possible now that you
Are deceived again? He's another flatterer. Think what it has cost

Us, for listening to fair words, and if we mind this one we will be lost.
We saw the gate from the mountain top ; by faith we onward must,
If we expect to happy be, and live amid the just.
Cease, Brother dear, I pray you cease from everything which will
Make you forsake the ways of truth and peace. If you fulfill
God's blest commands, you must resist all tempters, cease to hear
Him, and let us pursue our journey, or we will be punished, sure."
CHRIS. "You are right ; I did not ask the question of thee
Because I doubted the truth ; I only wished to see
What you would say. For this poor man, he is blinded by
This world. We must rejoice in the belief the soul can never die."
Then turned they from Atheist, and he went on his way.

➤✳ THE ENCHANTED GROUND. ✦ IGNORANCE. ✳⬅

HE pilgrims soon came into the Enchanted Ground, and
      Hopeful then did say,
   "Oh! Brother! I am sleepy now, can scarcely ope my eyes,
Suppose we take a nap right here."

                 CHRIS. "Alas! how quickly flies
All common sense! When passions blow the gale, let reason hold
    the helm ;
Remember the Enchanted Ground, and quickly wash the film
From off thine eyes."

            HOPE. "I confess I was all wrong ;
And I will try to prove more wise."

               And then they sang a song.
Then he sang : "When saints grow sleepy, let them come hither,
And hear how these pilgrims talked and sang together.
Let them hear how Satan tempted, and, fearing, grow wise
Enough to keep out of danger, and open their drowsy eyes.
Christian fellowship, if 'tis managed well,
Keeps them awake and shields from snares, as we can tell."
CHRIS. "Brother, what made you first think
Of forsaking sin ?"

         HOPE. "I knew I stood upon the brink
Of the precipice of ruin ; I continued in the delight
Of those things sold at Vanity's Fair ; each day and night
I added some new feature to my pleasures, and the wine
Had more charms for me than the beauties of a world divine ;
I delighted in rioting, Sabbath-breaking, all that tended
To destroy my soul. Ah! there was nothing good blended
With my feelings—but I heard how Faithful drew his latest breath
In prayer for his enemies. I knew my way was death;
I was convinced that sinners would reap eternal wrath ;
Yet I was loth to leave my companions, treading in sin's path.
I had so reckless been—to revert to my past gives me pain.
My prayers were not answered, and all to me seemed vain.
Then I had warning too, when I heard the tolling of the bell,

I knew not how soon it would be sounding my death-knell.
Thoughts like these pierced my heart, and continued to torment,
Until I determined I would follow Jesus, if it surely rent
Every friend from my bosom ; and praise God. From that day
I have felt happier, and will never cease to pray."
CHRIS. "I am glad you are no longer in the labyrinth of sin ;
Prayer is the door to heaven, and Faith the key to let us in."
HOPE. "Look behind us, is not that Ignorance I see ?"
CHRIS. "Yes ; perchance he may conclude to come and talk with
    thee."

      *   *   *   *   *   *

HOPE. "Friend, why dost thou loiter thus behind ?
Say, canst thou in our company some real pleasure find ?"
IGNORANCE. "I prefer my own thoughts to any one's talk,
I ever have the most sublime ideas when alone I walk."
CHRIS. "Will you be kind enough to let us have some of them ?
We believe in conversing with the most humble of men."
IGNOR. "I think of all to elevate, of God and heaven, and will leave
All of my old associates, and follow Christ—a blessing I'll receive."
CHRIS. "I'm doubtful of what you say, I see you're not aware
Of the trials which all undergo, and I fear you will never share
These blessings unless you change. Let me ask you, how you know
That you have left all things for God ?"
                               IGNOR. "My heart says so."
CHRIS. "The wise man says, ' he that trusteth his own heart
Is a fool,' and we dare not from his wise words depart."
IGNOR. "That is said of an evil man, I know that I am good."
CHRIS. "How can you prove this ? now it seems to me, each should
Be very careful, for God says, we are wicked and full of deceit,
That our righteousness is as filthy rags. I fear the heart's conceit.
IGNOR. "Tell me. Do you think I ever had a good thought ?
Yet I never in my life before, the mind of any one sought."
CHRIS. "Yes, a good heart has good thoughts, and that's a good life,
Which accords with God's commandments, but you should not have
    strife,
And know that you have these requisites, and not only think so."
IGNOR. "Pray tell me, what do you call a good life, and what assurance
Have we that we are living right ?"
                         CHRIS. "There are many kinds

Of acts by which we can distinguish the good, the heart which binds
Such confidence is seldom right

IGNOR. " What can be
Good thoughts concerning ourselves ?"

CHRIS. " Those which agree
With the word of God."

IGNOR. " When does each thought
Of ourselves agree with the word of God ?"

CHRIS. "Naught
Can we think of ourselves, 'tis when we pass only the
Same judgment as the Word does. I'll explain, and you can see
What the Word of God says of men in their ruined condition.
There is none righteous or doeth good, all would go into perdition,
If it was not for the blood of Christ. It saith also that the
Heart of man is evil from his youth, and now, when we
Think thus of ourselves, and feel guilty, it is then
Our thoughts are good, because they are not of men,
But according to God's commands."

IGNOR. " I never will
Believe that my heart is as yours."

CHRIS. " How cans't thou fulfill
What the Word of God requireth when thou never hadst even one
Correct thought concerning thyself ? I'll proceed, and when I'm done,
You can see your condition. As the Word passeth upon our heart,
So it passeth a judgment upon our ways, and we must depart
From every sin which it condemns, and when both heart and ways
    agree,
Then they are according to the Word."

IGNOR. " I cannot see
So through your dark meaning."

CHRIS. " And God's Word saith that man
Is sinful, and his ways are wrong ; and more, he never can
Enter life until he sees that he is desperately wicked ; when
He seeth thus, his sense returns ; but the generality of men
Are destitute of this humiliation. And these are, indeed, good
Thoughts, because they agree with God's Word. And now, friend,
    would
You like to know, also, what good thoughts are concerning
God ? "

IGNOR. " Certainly."

CHRIS. " When there is no discerning

Between our thoughts and what the Word of God emphatically
    commands,
When we think He is wiser than man, and then every one stands
Where they should in the sight of God. He cannot even abide
An egotistical person—remember the publican. We ne'er can hide
Any of our sins from Him."

                  IGNOR. "Do you think that I
Am so silly as to believe, that I can from His vengeance fly?
Or that I can ever be equal with Him, though I do my best?"
CHRIS. "Tell me, what do you think about it? Let me hear you, lest
I should condemn too rashly."

                  IGNOR. "I must
Look to Christ for justification, or I'll be forever thrust
From the presence of our God."

                  CHRIS. "How then thinkest thou?
Must believe in Christ, when thou dost not need Him; and how
Canst thou see the original infirmities and then be blind to see
The actual sins? Thy opinion of thyself doth render thee
Inconsistent. Thou hast never seen the necessity of Christ's power,
To justify thee before God. Thou hast never known the hour,
That thou wast willing to acknowledge thine actual need of Him."
IGNOR. "I believe notwithstanding, that I do not really sin
As much as you think I do."

                  CHRIS. "How dost thou believe?"
IGNOR. "That Christ died for sinners, and they shall not receive
His blessings unless they are, before God, justified from sin,
And Jesus by His merits will cause us to stand in Him."
CHRIS. "Le me give answer to this confession which I've heard,
Thou hast a fantastic faith, nowhere set forth in the Word,
Thy faith is false, because it takes God's gracious boon from thee,
Even the righteousness of Christ, and giveth it to yourself, you see,
This faith maketh not Christ a justifier of thy heart, but of thy
Actions, and of thy heart for action's sake, which is false, and by
So believing you yourself deceive, and unless you change, you will
Be left to meet the wrath of God. For, in order to fulfill
God's righteous law, we must for life unto our Saviour fly,
His sufferings have met the law, and he can well supply,
Our every need. In Him we hide, and sure if He presents
Us spotless to our Maker, for His sake God consents
To our acquittal from sin's doom."

                  IGNOR. "And must we then but trust
To what Christ did by his own death? If so, we surely thrust

Away every effort of our own, and this gives free, loose rein
To all our lusts ; we could then live just as we wish, if efforts are
    in vain ;
So it matters little how we act, for we may, as you think and say,
Be justified by Christ's shed blood, and all can, in this way,
Be cleansed from sin, if we but *believe it.*''

                    CHRIS. " Thy name
Is Ignorance: as thy name, so art thou, and everlasting disgrace
    and shame
Shalt thou reap. Ignorant thou art, of what righteousness is, or how
Man can appease the wrath of God, and I am sure that thou
Knowest naught of the truth in Christ. And thus I do believe
That you have never thought of it."

                   IGNOR. " 'Tis nonsense, and will receive
Full condemnation from the wise ; 'tis fanatic, and distracted,
And will cause great delusion, unless 'tis soon retracted."
HOPE. " Friend, Christ is so hid in God from the knowledge of us all,
That He cannot be known to us, unless by God revealed, and your fall
Into eternal death is sure, unless your heart is changed. For the
    power divine
Of God, to us must surely be revealed."

               IGNOR. "That's your belief, not mine ;
I have the majority on my side. I would blush an advocate to be
Of whims like yours ; the literati your absurdities all oppose, you see."
CHRIS. " Your heart, I know, is not all right, and you should not
    thus speak
Of such momentous matters. Now, sure, unless you seek
Jesus by faith, through the Father God, His face you ne'er can see.
The soul on Christ must lay its hold, and if right in His sight, faith
    must be
Wrought by the greatness of His power. Of this, I know that thou
Art ignorant. Be awakened! See thy error, oh! haste now
To remedy it. Go at once to the Lord Jesus ; by His grace alone
You can be saved. His righteousness, is God's. All has been done
By and through Him."

             Then Ignorance said: " You do go on so fast,
I cannot keep up with your arguments."

                He stopped, and they quick past
By him, and said : " Oh ! Ignorance, wilt thou so foolish be
As not to heed our counsel good, which we've twice given thee.
Alas ! unless you change, you will eventually know
Your dreadful fate when 'tis too late, and seeing the evil of doing so,

You'll remember the past when hope is gone. Reflect you now,
    and hear
The word of God by man to you, for thou hast much to fear.
But if you will in error still persist, you alone must be
The loser of eternal life. Oh, let my words warn thee."
Then Christian unto Hopeful said : "Brother, we are alone."
But I saw in my dream, though thus it seemed, one unto them had come
Heedless here and there he walked. It was Ignorance so poor.
And as he passed, they said, "What a pity that the door
Of perception is so closed to him; but there are many in his condition
They are blinded by conceit, and cannot be convinced that perdition
Awaits them every one. The Word says, ' He hath blinded their eyes
Lest they should see their fate.' What think you of a man who
    thus dies ? "
HOPE. " You are older than I am, I want your opinion, and then
I can form better conceptions."
                CHRIS. "I think that some men
Being naturally ignorant, do not know that such convictions tend
To their good, and therefore they persistently stifle, and thus send
Them forever from their minds, and flatter themselves in the way
Of their own hearts."
           HOPE. " I do certainly believe as you say."
CHRIS. " I know that I am right, without a doubt. So says the Word
The fear of the Lord is the beginning of wisdom ; but I too have heard
Some pretend to fear, without knowing what it was. True
Or right fear is discovered by three things, and if we pursue
The right course, we will commence at the first : By its rise :
It causes deep conviction for sin, and then it soon drives
The careworn soul to the feet of Christ for salvation. And this
Continueth in us a well of grace, and an unfailing source of bliss,
Makes the heart adore God, His Word keeping it humble, and making
It afraid to turn from Him. And we find it truly forsaking
Everything that would dishonor God, or grieve the blessed Spirit,
Or cause any to speak reproachfully of Jesus' precious merit."
HOPE. " You have said the truth ; with you I full agree. Have
    we passed
The Enchanted Ground ? "
          CHRIS. "Why? Don't you you wish this talk to last ? "
HOPE. " Oh! yes, I only thought I would like to know just where
We are."
    CHRIS. " We have two miles to go, and when we are there
We will rest. But let us resume our conversation. Now

The ignorant do not see themselves as they should, or how
They are influenced to stifle their feelings; they think such fear
Is of the devil, when 'tis of God. They resist it, and appear
Miserable unless they root out the last plant, when alas! Poor men,
They are the ones who lack in faith, and lacking this, they then
Become presumptuously confident, for these fears ever take
Away this terrible self-holiness, and cause us to forsake
Everything like dependence on G d. But we will take our leave
Of Ignorance, and his acts. I think, we can receive
Greater profit from another topic."

HOPE. "Suppose you lead the way."

— * * * * * *

CHRIS. "Do you know Mr. Temporary, who was forced, they say,
Into religious matters ?"

HOPE. "Yes, I know him, for he dwelt
In Graceless town, two miles from Honesty, and I think he felt
Very much attached to Turnback."

CHRIS. "You are right.
I remember he lived under the same roof, but he had once a sight
Of his sin, and was awakened to the wages which was due."
HOPE. "Yes, this was so ; for oft he has come asking which path he
must pursue."
CHRIS. "I do pity him, indeed. He told me once he did intend
To change, and go on pilgrimage, but suddenly I did offend.
I condemned his intimacy with Mr. Save-thy-Self, and then
He had no farther use for me."

HOPE. "May we not ask why men
Change so oft ?"

CHRIS. "In my judgment, there are reasons four.
The conscience of such as these is oftimes very sore,
From the practices of sin ; yet, their minds arn't thereby changed.
Therefore when the sense of guilt is gone, they find they are estranged
From their thoughts again, which makes them in a worse condition ;
And this is the way so many go, who end at last in perdition.
Some, under a religious excitement, have a great desire to do good,
But soon this passes off. and they become indifferent. We should
Ask God's help daily. Not doing this, we soon go back to our old
sins again.
The things of the world become our choice. To obey God is a shame ;

And their proud and haughty spirits are not willing now to bend
To the humble commands of God. And thus their way they wend
Back step by step to their old course. Guilt and terror favor them.
They do not like to see their misery beforehand, and these men
Shun all thought of the future, and harden their hearts madly."
CHRIS. "You are right; 'tis for the want of change, and sadly
They stand as stumbling blocks to others. The felon who receives
His doom, both quakes and trembles when he believes
The sentence of death is surely passed. But it is all the fear
Of the halter, and not penitence for his guilt and shame. He will
      appear
The same thief if acquitted, and if there is any change in his mind,
He would be otherwise."
                         HOPE. "And now can you find
The reason of their going back?"
                         CHRIS. "Yes; they do erase
All thoughts of God from out their mind, and soon they can retrace
Their steps. Their hearts have ne'er been changed; they soon begin
      to cast
Off private duties, and closet prayer, restraint of lust, and at last,
They shun the company of the good. Thus acting, they soon grow
Careless about their public life, turn from the Word, and show
Feelings of envy—finding fault with others who do wrong,
Urging they cannot stay with hypocrites—and many throng
Daily to them, saying, 'I have seen church members do such things
As would disgrace a moral man, such conduct always brings
To my mind, a disgust for religion.' But should they not despise
The men, and not religion? When they thus speak, the last spark flies
From them, and they will seek the company of wanton men;
They are much worse than e'er before, and are always glad, when
Those who are considered honest, act wrong, that they may the more
Boldly do it, through their example. But ah! when this life is o'er,
How will they stand before the Bar?"

➤✳ THE BEULAH LAND. ✳←

SAW that by this time,
  They had passed the Enchanted Ground, and all things
    seemed divine
For they were inspired with a new life; and incessantly they heard
The rippling of some crystal stream, and the song of some glad bird,
As it winged to some sequestered bower, whose rich and rare perfume
Made sweet, as Araby the Blest, the balmy air of noon.
The pilgrims haste, and soon they gain the lovely Beulah's land.
Now they can rest, and be refreshed, for here God's gracious hand
Had lavished beauties without stint. Here there is no more night;
The Shining Ones walk grandly here, forever in the sight
Of the Blest City, and 'tis here the Bridegroom and the Bride
United are in lasting bonds. Here endless joys abide.
For as the Bridegroom rejoiceth over the Bride, so doth God
Rejoice over pilgrims dear, who have come the narrow road.
And as they wended on their way, they now and then could hear
Voices from the City, which in glimpses did appear.
They listed to the music sweet. 'Twas daughters of Zion. "Behold!
  behold!
Thy salvation cometh. Reward you will reap." They lovingly were told
Here, that they were the redeemed of the Lord, whom He Himself had
  sought
Out as His own. What pleasure these sweet words to their ears
  brought!
And as they drew the City near, they had a grander view:
'Twas built of pearls; its streets of gold, its beauties ever new.
How meagre now their trials were, in contrast to their joy!
Their troubles had worked out for them pleasure without alloy.
And as they pressed along their way, rich vineyards, glad and fair,
Scattered o'er the flowered plains, were fruits of all kinds rare.
They asked, " Whose vineyards are these, friend?" The man replied:
                                                        "The King's.
They are planted for the Pilgrim's food, while of His Lord he sings.
Here beauteous birds, with matin throat, and all kinds of fruits
  are kept

For Pilgrim's cheer. Here are rich bowers. Walk in."

And so they slep
And were refreshed with peace and strength. Now saw I in my dream
That they talked much while sleeping, and this to me did seem
Most strange.

The man replied their grapes caused this effect; they
Had heard many speak in their sleep, and often they would say
Things lofty and sublime to hear.

After resting, the pilgrims proceed
On their journey, but the reflection of the City made them need
An instrument to behold its effulgence. Meeting with two men,
Whose raiments shined like unto gold, " Oh ! tell us, how and when
Our way to make ? "

They said : " Of trials you but have two more
To encounter, ere you will be through."

The friends were very sore,
And well nigh lost their faith. Then they asked them again,
About the way, and wanted their company. They told them :

" To obtai
Eternal joy, you sure must go along with faith alone."

➤✳ THE RIVER OF DEATH. ✳⬅

THE gate is in sight,
Yet there lay between them and the City, a River.
Ah!—the night
Of deep despair, which o'ershades many when they come to this
River of Death!
But this is the only way which leads to the home of eternal breath,
The pilgrims asked the men, if through this dark river,
Was the only way to the gate ? And if some one could not deliver
Them from this trial ? They told them that only two men had ever
Found any other way: Enoch and Elijah. And now they must sever
Every tie, and only have faith. Then Christian began to despond,
And looked in every direction for escape. At the river, they found
Guides encouraging them to have faith, for the waters were not deep.
Then they went in, and began to sink. Poor Christian could not keep
His head above water; he cried: "The billows are over my head!"
"Be of good cheer, the bottom is good. Come on!" brave Hopeful
said.
But he despairingly answered back: "The sorrows of death do
compass me round"
I can ne'er see the goodly land, but God's frown
Will be upon me. All is darkness, I ne'er shall behold the face
Of my Redeemer!"
HOPE. "He is able, with His saving grace,
To carry you safely through."
CHRIS. "Oh! the sins I have done,
Can never be forgiven! I will remain here, and you alone,
Will reap the reward of the blest."
HOPE. "I see the gate,
And men standing to receive us!"
CHRIS. "No! 'Twill be my fate
To perish here, many sins have brought me in this snare ;
Oh! Why was I so wicked?"
HOPE. "Remember your Record, where
The Psalmist says, the wicked have no fears of death,
But their strength is firm, they defy God in their last breath.

These troubles are no sign that God has refused your prayers, or
    forsaken
You, but are sent to test your faith; I know that you are mistaken
In your fearful apprehensions."

                  Christian was silent. Hopeful said, "Be
Of good cheer, Christ will make thee whole."

                        CHRIS. "Ah! I see
Him now! And hear Him say, ' When thou passeth through
The waters, they shall not o'erflow thee.'—Yes, all is true,
He said He would be my comfort and strength."

                        HOPE. " I told thee
To be encouraged."

        Now Christian found bottom, and said, " I see
Some one on the opposite side ! "

➤✳ MOUNT ZION. ✳◄

AND there were waiting, two men,
    To welcome all, as they came out of the river. They
       salute them,
Saying, they are ministering spirits, sent forth to minister to the heirs
Of salvation. Now they went towards the gate with few fears,
For they led them by the arms; and they ascended the hill with ease,
For they had left their mortal garments in the river, and these
Men assisted them on, so they went with joy and speed.
Though the foundation of the City was higher than the clouds, they
    had no need
That any man assist them, but went, sweetly talking, through the air.
They had passed "The River" safely, and with heavenly company rare
They were delighted. Their talk was of the glory of the place,—
Mount Zion—the heavenly Jerusalem, where they could see the face
Of their blessed Saviour.
              " In the paradise of God, you'll see
Innumerable angels, and the never fading-flowers, and eat of the Tree
Of Life; and you shall have white robes given you, and your
    daily walk
Shall be with the King himself. Through eternal ages you will talk
Of His majesty and grace. No sorrow or death can ever come,
For old things have passed away. The joy of your bright home
Is indeed beyond description. Abraham and Jacob are there,
And the prophets, with many redeemed of the Lord. They will
    prepare
To receive you. Here, reward will be given for pain and toil,
There will be pleasures for your troubles, and though Satan tried
    to foil
You in every effort, you still kept on. And now with praise,
And thanksgiving, you shall spend an eternity of days.
There you shall join your friends who have before you gone.
When Jesus comes again, and the sin-cursed earth is shorn
Of all her vanity and crime, you shall have a voice
'Gainst all who have oppressed you. Filled with love, you will rejoice
Over all you trials past. Here you will dwell in peace forever
With the happy and the blest. No touch of death shall sever
This unalloyed tie."

* * * * * *

And, lo! a heavenly host came to meet them,
Whom the Shining Ones said, "See these men. You must greet them
With a warm and welcome kiss, for they have left all for God's name,
And we have brought them thus far, and now the glorious fame
Of their mansion will be seen."

Then they gave a shout, long and loud,
Saying: "Blessed are they who are called to the Marriage
Supper." When a cloud
Of brightness o'ershadowed them; the air reverberated with the
melody
Of their voices. They never thought this happiness they should see.
It appeared all of the heavenly hosts had come to meet them,
and as they did behold,
Their hearts pulsed with love. They said they had ne'er been told
Of this great happiness they would have. And now, as they
sweetly sing,
The fair City comes in view, and they hear the loud bells ring,
To welcome them at home. But above all was the joyful thought
Of being eternally with such friends, and in their souls this wrought
Such gratitude and love, they knew not what to think. Then
they came
To the gate over which was written, in letters of gold, the name
Of the City; and these lines:

"Blessed Are They Who Have Obeyed Each Command."

* * * * * *

Christian said to Hopeful, "Knock! We will in our King's presence
stand."
Then I saw in my dream the heavenly host. And the massive gate
of pearl
On golden hinges open flew. Angels their banners did unfurl,
To welcome the pilgrims home. They joined the choral symphonies,
Saying, "Hosanna to the Highest, we now rest from enemies."

*   *   *   *   *   *

DRAW aside the curtain. Hold it with the star of morn.

     Let the beautiful echo from heaven

Resound through the earth, 'til by her peoples new-born, all power

    unto God shall be given.

FRAGMENTS.

A Scene at the Palace of the High Priests.

PRIESTS. What darkness! Will he never come? How late!
A few hours more, and all is over. Lo! our fate
Depends upon prompt action.- -'Tis footsteps I hear.
CAPTAIN. The lamp glimmers ; a low figure doth appear. (*Enter Judas*).
The time for avenging will soon expire,
This night we must vent our long-pent ire.
Look to the weapons,—lanterns. Ah! how time flies!
Ah! nevermore his name be wafted to the skies!

*   *   *   *   *   *

Near the Mount of Olives.

[*Christ and His Disciples.*]

CHRIST. We will go to the Mount of Olives to pray,
That we may be guided in the right way.
(*Alone*) I see an angel, sweet messenger of love,
Sent to cheer me, from my Father above.
My soul is exceeding sorrowful, even unto death—
Nature sympathizes ; Heaven holds her breath.
(*Prays.*) Father! If it be Thy will, let this cup pass from me,
Yet I came into the world to glorify Thee. (*Returns to disciples.*)
Alas, how weak! Could not watch an hour—all asleep!
Is this your devotion? What vigils ye doth keep!
Awake now, awake! See how Judas now doth stand,
Demon-like, with his dark and blood-thirsty band ;
My blood will soon be spilt, to purge sin away,
But from it will spring a bright, undying day,
To shine o'er this dark and sin-polluted world ;
Henceforth, my banner of love shall be unfurled.

[*Judas with the multitude approaches—the disciples scatter.*]

JUDAS. 'Tis him whom I kiss ; lay hold on him and bind.
JESUS. Betrays't thou the Son of Man with a kiss? Oh! malice
undefined !

(*To the Chief Priests*) Come ye out as against a thief, with swords
    and with staves?
I could pray my Father, and receive legions from heaven's concaves.
I was with you in the Temple, and daily in your power,—
But the prophecies must be fulfilled. Improve your passing hour.

> [*Simon Peter draws a sword against the High Priest's servant and
> cuts off his ear.*]

PETER. If it costs my life I will defend my Master. Wretch, beware!
JESUS. Put up thy sword, I drink this cup; to me there is no fear.
CHIEF CAPTAIN. Come soldiers! do your duty now, and bind the
    deceiver fast.
You seem amazed! Be at your work, this dalliance must not last.

    *   *   *   *   *   *

IN THE HIGH PRIEST'S PALACE.

(*Enter Judas.*) Here, take your money! 'Tis the price of innocent
    blood!
His calm, sweet face, it haunts me now; my grief, an angry flood,
O'erwhelms my soul. I'm lost! I'm lost! Oh! let me hide my face;
Hell's gaping fiends are all about. Disgraced! I'm sure disgraced!
For thirty pieces of silver I the Lord of Life betrayed.
Oh, why did I this horrid deed? This dreadful blunder made,
The fatal knot around my neck I will myself go tie,
And like a loathsome traitor die, for I deserve to die.
CHIEF PRIESTS. Take the mock king to the High Priests; there let
    him pray,
And now perchance his prayer may be answered on the way.
PETER. I'll never betray my Master, the last of Him I will see.

> [*Damsel asks Peter if he is not a disciple.*]

PETER. Indeed I'm not. I came, and this is all of me.

> [*An officer says: " Thou art one of them."*]

PETER. And do you not believe me? Then my answers are in vain.
I have denied this thrice, and why need I now again?

> [*The cock crows, and Peter remembers the word of the Lord.*]

PILATE. What has this poor man done? His guilt I cannot see.
PRIESTS. He is a malefactor, or would have not sent to thee.

[Pilate taketh Jesus unto the Judgment Hall.]

PILATE. We are now all alone. Now tell me, art thou King ?
JESUS. Of thyself, or some other, askest thou this thing.
PILATE. Knoweth thou of what the Chief Priests thee accuse ?
JESUS. I'm not of this world. For this they me accuse.

[Pilate asks again if He is King.]

JESUS. For this end I came into this sinful world.
Some hear me, and accept all ; others shall be hurled
Into everlasting woe—the gulf of dark despair.
Too late ! will be their wail ; unheeded then their prayer.

[Pilate goeth out, and tries to influence the Jews.]

PILATE. This man is innocent, and he is the King of the Jews.
MULTITUDE. Oh ! what will Cæsar say ? Thou darest not refuse.

[Pilate returns to Jesus, and scourges Him.]

PILATE. It pains me thus to scourge you, man. I would not do you ill.
But I am in their hands to-day, and must their wish fulfill.

[A band of soldiers enter.]

CAPT. Put this crown of thorns upon his vile head,
And here's a royal robe. Think what the impostor said.

*[All cry out in one voice: " Hail ! Master ! King ! Blindfold Him, and
let Him tell who smote His honored face."]*

PILATE *(to the Jews)*. I cannot condemn, for I find no fault in him.
I've examined closely, and find he has not sinned.

[All cry out: Crucify ! crucify Him !]

JEWS. Only think ! a man to make himself God's Son !
PILATE. I know that he is innocent. Alas ! what can be done ?
PILATE'S WIFE. Have thou nothing to do with this just person.
This man is not guilty, last night I had such dream
And my head is o'er burdened, such mysteries o'er it teem.
*[Pilate goeth into the Judgment Hall and saith unto Jesus : Whence art
thou ?—Jesus remains silent].*

PILATE. Why this silence ? refusest thou to speak to me ?
I have power to condemn, or power to set thee free.
JESUS. All power you possess, is given thee from above.
I pity all, their bitter sneers doth not my anger move.
PILATE *(to Jesus)*. All of my efforts to release you are in vain. *(unto
the Jews)* Behold ! Your king !

JEWS. We have no king save Cæsar. Let this fellow die.
PILATE (*to Jesus*). List to what they say, " Crucify him, crucify!
Give unto us Barabbas!" Ah! soon the day will come
When you, denied repentance, will stand to meet your doom.
JEWS (*to Pilate*). We fear not. Let His blood be on us and children
forever.
Refuse Him now to us, and you shall feel our ire.
You boast your power; come tell us now art thou Cæsar's friend ?
If so, how dost thou dare in this your ruler to offend ?
PILATE. Why not take Barabbas, the murderer and thief?
SOLDIERS. No! Place this crown upon His head, and call Him mighty
Chief,
Spit in his face, and mock Him, too, and strike Him with a reed,
Aha! Aha! His royal robe He will no longer need.
CAPT. (*unto Simon.—Simon tries to escape*). Come hither man, this
traitor's cross to bear.
And should you dare refuse, his fate you soon will share.
JESUS (*seeth a company of women-weeping, and saith unto them*) :
Weep for yourselves and children—weep not for me.
My sufferings shall be brief; soon my glory you will see.
They will cry for mercy, and that mountains on them fall,
And hide them from sure vengeance, but their anguished call
Will be in vain. Are we now to Calvary ?
CAPT. Then we can hear more of this great mystery.
Crucify one thief on his left, the other on his right—
The King between two malefactors. Ah! the sight.

*   *   *   *   *   *

CHIEF PRIESTS. Lay Him on the cross, and nail His majestic hands.
JESUS. Father, forgive them; they do not understand.
PEOPLE. Dost thou destroy and build the Temple in three days ?
Come from the cross, and then we'll give Thee praise.
ONE OF THE THIEVES. If Thou be God, save Thyself and us from
this degradation.
OTHER THIEF. We're guilty, He is not, yet in the same condemnation !
Lord, when Thou comest unto Thy Kingdom, will Thou think of me ?
JESUS. Thou art now forgiven; this day my glory Thou shalt see.
HOLY WOMEN. Hope of Israel, we know Thou art pure and divine.
Lo! the earth trembles; the sun forgets to shine.
Flashes of lightning, and a dark cloud for His frown,
From which torrents of rain fall, for He hides His crown.

JESUS. Father, into Thy hand my spirit I now commend.
CENTURION. He is righteous. God will His vengeance send.
JOSEPH OF ARIMATHEA (to Pilate). Wilt thou let me take my Saviour's
body out of sight?
NICODEMUS. Here are spices—I came to worship Him by night.
JOSEPH. In this new sepulchre man never has been laid.
WOMEN. Let us get spices—remember the Sabbath, as He said.

* * * * * *

THE CHIEF PRIESTS AND PHARISEES AT PILATE'S PALACE.

CHIEF PRIESTS (to Pilate.) The deceiver said, after three days He
would rise again,
And His crucifixion may yet be in vain,
For His disciples can deceive; we know that they will say
That He is risen, when they have stolen Him away.
PILATE. Go and make your guard attend to it. Have Him secure
By sealing the stone; and by this means His body will be sure.

* * * * * *

SOLDIERS AROUND THE SEPULCHRE.

1st SOLDIER. He saved others, and seemed to prove Himself divine,
Yet He failed in not saving Himself. Pass the wine.
2nd SOLDIER. Look above! See an angel, I'm filled with deep fear;
How plainly now our sin we see! As day it doth appear.
[Angel appeareth and hovereth o'er the tomb.—The soldiers fall back in
dismay.—The Angel rolleth the stone away.]
ANGEL. Death has no power over God's holy Son.
JESUS (rising). I rise in might and glory. Father, Thy work is done.
ANGEL. Look where they laid Him, but He's not here.
Think what He said. This will not strange appear.

Jesus secludes himself behind some shrubs.—The soldiers flee into Jerusalem.—Mary Magdalene cometh to the sepulchre with the mother of
James].

MARY M. I'm filled with fear. Whose form is that I see?
MARY. My feelings I could not tell to thee.
JESUS. Why those downcast looks? Whom seekest thou?
MARY. My crucified Saviour, before whose throne I bow.

Hast thou taken Him away? Shall I ne'er see Him more?
MARY M. We will meet Him again on that celestial shore.
JESUS. Mary! go tell my brethren I must soon ascend.
MARY. Rabbi! the prophecies of Thy resurrection here do end.
MARY M. Come with me. Remember our Saviour said
To His disciples, before His crucifixion, that He would rise from
the dead.
[*While the disciples are talking, Jesus draweth near.*]
JESUS. Tell me why this sadness, as onward ye do walk?
CLEOPAS. The crucifixion of Jesus, it is now all the talk.
Some women, going early to His sepulchre, have seen
Angels, who said He had risen, as strange as it doth seem.
JESUS. Do you not believe the prophets? Let me explain
Certain passages, list! Let it not be in vain;
DISCIPLE. Come with us, glad to have you spend the night.
[Christ goes, and eats with them, them vanishes from sight.]
SIMON PETER. We ought to have known Him, by His blessing of the
bread,
Why do you not think on all that I have said?
CHRIST (*Appeareth*). About my death and resurrection, behold now
my feet
And hands, hath a spirit flesh? Bring me now to eat;
It was written, by the prophets, that Christ shall rise,
And soon I must ascend from earth unto the skies,
Teach, baptize, and with these, my doctrines ever blend.
Obey me, and lo! I am with you e'en unto the end.

*　　　　*　　　　*　　　　*　　　　*　　　　*

AT THE SEA OF TIBERIAS.

[*The disciples fishing.—Christ appeareth.*]
JESUS. Cast your net on the right side, and you then shall find.
PETER. 'Tis the Lord! My Lord! My coat around me I'll bind,
And go to him. My Master! I knew it was thee.
JESUS. Look! see the fish they have, a hundred and fifty-three.
(*To disciples.*) There is bread and fish, in full, now come and with
me dine.
Remember how I've been seen of you, this the third time.
Tarry until I send you power from on high.
Weep not for me! In heaven there is not e'en a sigh.
DISCIPLES. Look! Angels are coming to welcome Him home.
JESUS. Father, my work is finished. To Thee I come! I come!

THE LIFE OF STEPHEN AND PAUL,

WITH TWO IMAGINARY CHARACTERS PAULINA AND NEITA.

→✳ DEATH OF STEPHEN. ✳←

STEPHEN. Lena, I am selected to administer to the poor and widows.

LENA. I want you to be useful, but I feel like some evil will soon befall you. Sadness, like a dark shroud, has spread his chilling folds around me, and I cannot rend them away by prayer.

STEPHEN. I hope this is a mere mist of gloom, which will vanish when the sun of reason arises.

LENA Would I could think so. But when our utmost duty is done, we must welcome what we cannot shun.

STEPHEN. If I knew I had to sacrifice my life, I would not swerve from my duty; for, the spider's most attenuated thread, is cable to man's hold on earthly bliss. It breaks at every breath, I know my enemies are numerous, and threats have been made against my life; yet, the greatest sorrow which pierces my heart, is your grief; if I could only mitigate that, death would lose its sting. And I must soon leave you. Be cheerful; as our days are, so shall our strength be.

LENA. I dread my brother's vengeance. He is the worst enemy you have, though he knows my attachment for you.

STEPHEN. He is indeed an influential man. Would that his zeal was for Christ and his cause.

[*A company of horsemen approach.*]

LENA. Oh! I hear the rapid tramp of horses. Escape! I knew they would arrest you.

STEPHEN. We will be happy in yonder world.

LENA. Do not lose your life in talking to me, remember the trap door.

[*Stephen vanishes, men rush into the room.*]

CAPT. Where have you hid him? (*Lena remains silent*).

SAUL. Sister, answer the Chief Captain, or your life will be a forfeit for his.

LENA. Let them torture me, but never, no never will I betray him!

CAPT. Proceed at once, and test her heroism.

SOLDIERS. We came here to arrest a man, and not one so fair.

STEPHEN. (*rushes in*). The first one who approaches her shall die! I am now your prisoner. What accusations have you against me?

CAPT. You must answer before the Council.

STEPHEN. I am prepared to answer both before an earthly, and a heavenly tribunal.

STEPHEN (*aside to Paulina*). Weep not for me: each sigh is like a dagger to my heart. I will be the first martyr. What a glorious death! Many others will follow. Dry your tears, we will soon meet again.

CAPT. Bind that man, he talked enough before we came, he will not have much use for love when we get through with him.

STEPHEN. Go into another room, dear.

LENA. Oh, let me die with you! I cannot leave you thus!

STEPHEN. Paulina, have fortitude. Good-bye.

1st. WITNESS. I heard him say that our temple should be destroyed. He denies our faith and adheres to an imposter's doctrine. I have heard him blaspheme the word of God.

2nd WIT. He does not believe in Moses, and says all of our customs shall be changed.

[*A bright light o'ershadows Stephen.*]

HIGH PRIEST. Are these things so?

STEPHEN. Brethren, you know I believe in Abraham, Moses and all the prophets—but which of them escaped your fathers' wrath? You have slain those who foretold the birth of Jesus, of whom ye have been the betrayers and murderers. Do not gnash your teeth; the truth pricks to the heart; your guilt is open to all.

PEOPLE. Away with him! Will he cast his insults in our face?

LENA (*rushes to Saul*). Oh! Brother, do try to rescue him! My God! My heart is bursting!

NEITA (*Friend to Lena*). Behold! How they all gaze on his countenance! That radiance is the reflection of the crown which the angel of Hope holds o'er his head.

SAUL. Lena, speak!

NEITA. Has she fainted ?

SAUL. Oh! she is dead. Alas! were the pangs so great as to burst life's tender chords asunder ? Ah! the nearest tie is severed, but I will avenge myself of her destroyer.

HIGH P. He has condemned himself, and deserves stoning.

SAUL. Give me his clothes.

HIGH P. All you throw stones at him!

STEPHEN. Lord Jesus, receive my spirit, and lay not this sin to their charge.

SAUL (*To the High Priest*). I want authority to bind both men and women, in Damascus.

PRIEST. My son, we have few so zealous as thyself. Take as many with thee as thou desirest."

A bright light o'ershadows him, and he hears a voice, saying:

Saul! Saul! Why persecutest thou me ?

Saul trembles and falls to the ground, asking

Lord, what wilt thou have me to do?

VOICE. Arise and go into the city, and it shall be told thee what thou shalt do.

MEN. Oh! Saul! explain this mystery! We heard the voice—saw the light—yet no man was visible.

SAUL. It was the voice of Jesus! Lead me to Damascus. Oh, tell my aged parents of this change; what joy it will give them! Would that Lena were alive, to share it, too. May you all feel as I do.

JUDAS. Brother Saul, you have not eaten anything in three days, let me insist on you having some refreshment.

SAUL. I am too much o'erwhelmed with grief—am beholding myself in the mirror of the past, and can well exclaim, Oh! Memory! That mirror which affliction dashes to the ground, and on looking down, only beholds its fragments multiplied!

JUDAS. Brother, do not fall into the Slough of Despond, though your head be bowed down, with grief, you shall lift it in power.

SAUL. I can see deeds darker than midnight—can hear the echoes of Lena's dying voice, "Spare! oh, spare my Stephen to me!" Then methinks I see Stephen, with his forgiving smile, and radiant brow, and I, demon-like, holding the clothes.

JUDAS. Drop the curtain of the past, and look to the future.

SAUL. I have seen in a vision Ananias coming unto me.
JUDAS. It is the Lord's doings, obey him.

ANANIAS IN DAMASCUS.

A VOICE IN THE NIGHT. Go to the house of Judas, for, Behold! Saul prayeth there.

ANANIAS. Lord, I have heard of this man. He has authority to bind all believers at this place.

LORD. Go thy way; he shall be a chosen vessel before me to the Gentiles, and suffer many things for my sake.

ANANIAS. Brother Saul, I have come to tell thee to receive thy sight, and be filled with the Holy Ghost.

SAUL. I am willing to serve my Lord in any way. I believe He has forgiven me.

ANANIAS. Arise and be baptized, and fulfill His commands.

PAUL. Oh! Lord, give me strength; the spirit is willing, but the flesh is weak.

SIMON, LUCAS AND MARCUS. Now Brother, depart in peace, and may God bless your labors.

PAUL AND BARNABAS IN SALAMIS.

SERGIUS PAULUS. My friends, will you explain to me the Word of God, and what I must do to be saved?

PAUL. You are familiar with the prophets, and if you search them diligently, you will find they all testify of Christ being the Son of God, and of the death he should die; that He would rise again, and sit on the right hand of God, to make intercession for sinners. It is through Him our sins are pardoned.

ELYMAS *unto Sergius.* You are talking to a fanatic. The High Priests read all the prophets. The impostor Christ, denied all we believe, and said the temple should be destroyed and built again in three days.

PAUL. Thou child of the devil, and enemy to all righteousness, wilt thou never cease to prevent the way of the Lord? Behold! His hand is upon thee, and thou shalt be blind for a season.

ELYMAS. I have sinned. Send some one to lead me.

SERGIUS. I know this power you possess comes from God. I do believe with all my heart, and want to follow my Saviour,

and may every one feel the same bliss I do, in acknowledging
His mercy.

PAUL. May God bless you, my brother, and help you to hold
fast to His precious promises.

PAUL AT ANTIOCH, IN PERSIDIA.

[*Addresses the Multitude.*]

MEN AND BRETHREN :—Ye who fear the Lord give audience.
God with a strong arm brought our forefathers out of Egypt.
They dwelt forty years in the wilderness, and He destroyed
seven nations for them, and gave them judges one hundred
and fifty years, until Samuel the prophet. After him, they
desired a king, and God gave them Saul for forty years. Then
He removed him, and made David king,—of whom He said he
was a man after His own heart. Of this man's seed hath God,
according to His promise, raised unto Israel a Saviour—Jesus.
John preached the baptism of repentance, and said, "There
cometh one after me, whose shoes I am not worthy to unloose."
And to you who fear God is this salvation sent, but your rulers
knew Him not, for they have fulfilled the prophets in condemn-
ing Him. They found no fault in Him, yet they desired He
should be slain, and after He was crucified, God raised Him
from the dead. And now He sitteth on His right hand, making
intercession for sinners, and by Him, all who believe are justified. Beware! Remember what the prophets said, "Ye shall
perish! for I work, and ye shall in no wise believe."

GENTILES *unto Paul.* Wilt thou preach the same sermon
next Sabbath ?

PAUL. I am a servant, and will do anything to change your
wicked ways.

JEWS *unto Paul and Barnabas.* The Gentiles' request has
been complied with, and we the chosen people of God are not
noticed.

PAUL. It was necessary the Word should be preached to
you, but you have rejected it, and lo! we turn to the Gentiles.

JEWS. We know you were trying to overthrow our doctrine.

CHIEF CAPTAIN. Drive these fanatics from hence.

A GENTILE. They preached unto you first, and your hearts
were hardened—but we have received them gladly. God says
they shall be a light unto us, and we believe it is beyond your
power to extinguish one of their dimmest rays.

PAUL DEPARTETH TO ICONIUM.

CHIEF PRIEST. We must away with these disturbers, or our creed will be lost. Stir up the discontented and have them stoned.

A FRIEND *unto Paul.* Do you not know that the whole city is gathering, to stone you? Flee! We will assist you in making your escape.

PAUL. The Lord is on our side.

BARNABAS. This is a dark, rainy night, they will never dream of our leaving. Our friends must not know of our going.

CITY OF ICONIUM IN AN UPROAR.

CHIEF CAPTAIN *unto Chief Priests.* I commanded these officers to keep a close watch over those men, but I fear they have let a little rain prevent them from performing their duty.

CAPTAIN *unto Officer.* Search diligently for them, and if they cannot be found, I will hold you responsible.

OFFICER. They are not in the city, but we will have them as soon as they can be brought.

CHIEF CAPTAIN *unto Officer.* Where are your prisoners?

OFFICER. At Lystra, performing such miracles as never man performed before. They healed a man who had been lame from his birth, and all they did was to command him to stand on his feet; and the people say, that the gods have come down in the likeness of men. They call Paul Jupiter, and Barnabas Mercurius. They brought oxen and garlands and wanted to sacrifice to them, but these holy men of God stopped them, and said God alone should be worshiped, and they must turn from such vanities; but they could scarcely restrain them.

CHIEF PRIEST. I knew we would be ruined. Put the bearer of this unwelcome news in prison, and send others and see if they will be converted too.

OFFICER. If they see what I did, they will be convinced that our religion is like a whited sepulchre.

HIGH PRIESTS. Dare you speak thus after refusing to obey our orders!

PAUL AND BARNABAS AT LYSTRA.

PAUL. Look, Brother! there is a company from Iconium! We will be arrested, for they have imprisoned the other officer because he believed on God. We cannot do more for Christ than He has done for us. I am prepared for the worst.

Officers and Man Approach.

Where are those men who disturb our peace?

PEOPLE. There is the principal one.

PAUL. I am here willing to suffer for my Master's cause. Oh! ye fickle-minded men of Lystra, ye are among our enemies too, only a few days ago and you would have worshiped us—gods one day, and demons the next.

CAPT. Why do you all stand listening? Stone him! he deserves death. [*All cast stones*].

PAUL. Oh! Lord, I thank Thee I am worthy to suffer for Thy name. They can kill my body, but my soul will live in endless peace.

CAPT. He is dead. Drag him out of the city. Where is the other? Does it take a whole town and company to kill one man?

SOLDIERS. Barnabas has escaped while we were slaying Paul.

CAPT. We have the one who has done the most mischief; let us return at once and report to the High Priests.

[*Paul's friends gather around him to see if there are any signs of life.*]

PRISCILLA. His pulse beats! He breathes! Bring some water. Ah! His lips move, Oh God spare him! We had better take him to the nearest house, and bathe his bruised limbs, we may be discovered here. How he suffers!

PAUL. Do not fear; I am better now, and thankful I can suffer for Thy cause, O God!

DISCIPLE. Do not talk, we must conceal you; the Jews think you are dead.

PAUL. God gives me strength. I can see poor Stephen how he looked on his enemies. Forgiveness beamed from his face, and his last breath was a prayer for them, he is now in glory, and I am here to suffer.

DISCIPLE. Dear brother, we will do all we can to alleviate

your pain. Bathe your bruised limbs, and sleep, refreshing sleep will soon soothe you.

BARNABAS. Brother, I would not have left you, but I knew I could be of no service. They must have thought we are the sons of Sampson from the number that tried to arrest us. When I escaped I never expected to see you in this world. We must go to Derbe, or we will be detected.

AT EPHESUS.

DISCIPLE (*unto Paul*). How long did you stay at Derbe?

PAUL. Only a few days, but we strengthened the brethren, and felt benefited ourselves. Have you received the Holy Ghost?

DISCIPLE. We have not so much as heard that there is a Holy Ghost.

PAUL. Unto what were ye baptized, then?

DIS. Unto John's baptism.

PAUL. John baptized unto repentance, saying, that one should come after him—Jesus Christ—who would send the Holy Ghost as a comforter, after He ascended into heaven.

DIS. We will be baptized in the name of the Lord. There are twelve of us, and we will assist you all we can.

PAUL. I see fruit of the seed sown by the Spirit. And now, brethren, we will lay our hands on you, and you will receive the Holy Ghost.

TIMOTHEUS (*unto Paul*). Since I have been traveling with you I feel like all things have become new, and though trials may await me, I have a power from on high to sustain me through them all.

PAUL. I am glad to hear you express yourself in that way, for last night I saw a man in a vision, saying, "Come over and help us!" And as we are needed at Macedonia, we will start immediately.

PAUL. Our trip has been so pleasant that I can hardly realize we are in Macedonia, where prayer is wont to be made. Ah! I see quite a number of women resorting hither.

LYDIA (*after preaching*). My mind is clear, my heart is changed, and to add to my joy, my entire household have expressed a desire to unite with God's people.

PAUL. It always affords me much pleasure to comply with such requests.

[*A damsel who brought her master much gain by sooth-saying, followeth Paul and Silas.*]

DAMSEL. These men are servants of the Most High God, which shew us the way of salvation.

PAUL (*unto the spirit*). I command thee in the name of Jesus Christ to come out of her. (*Unto Silas*) Behold the multitude! Be prepared.

DEMETRIUS. How dare you interfere with my profits? Arrest these men and bring them before the magistrates.

MULTITUDE. We testify that these men are disturbers of the peace, and teach customs which are not lawful for us to receive.

MAGISTRATE. Beat them severely, and charge the jailor to put them in the darkest dungeon.

A SCENE AT THE JAIL AT MIDNIGHT.

PRISONER. Ah! List! Did you ever hear such music? Surely heaven hath spared some of the celestial host to cheer this loathsome place.

ANOTHER PRISONER. Why are you shaking so?

1st. PRIS. It is not me but the earth. Lo! Look at the doors, they are all open, yet we dare not escape.

[*The jailor awaketh and draweth a sword to kill himself.*]

PAUL. Do thyself no harm, we are all here.

JAILOR. Give me a light. I now know that I have sinned, and while I prostrate myself to the ground, tell me what I must do to be saved.

PAUL. Believe on the Lord Jesus Christ and thou shalt be saved.

JAILOR. Let me bathe your stripes. Will you forgive me, and baptize me and mine, as we are all convinced that we are wrong, and you are right?

PAUL. Arise and be baptized.

JAILOR. Never was night so pregnant with good—you have ministered unto us such spiritual food as we needed; now come into my house and be refreshed physically.

PAUL. We are more than compensated, that good has resulted from our suffering. Often, troubles are blessings in disguise.

SERGEANTS (*unto Jailor*. Let these men go.

KEEPER (*unto Paul*). The magistrates say you can have your freedom.

PAUL. They have beaten us openly, and uncondemned, and it is beneath a Roman to be thrust out privily.

SERGEANTS (*unto Magistrates*). Those men refuse to depart unless you liberate them openly.

MAGISTRATES. We may get into trouble and must be more careful in the future. [*Unto Paul and Silas*]. We beseech you to depart in peace, and regret the measures we have taken; only leave us, and we will be more guarded.

PAUL AND SILAS IN THESSALONICA.

PAUL [*in the Synagogue*]. I love to dwell on my Saviour's love, how he came as an innocent babe, suffered and died, and rose again, and is now on the right hand of God, pleading for lost sinners.

JASON (*whispers to Paul*). Your life is in danger; certain lewd Jews have lit the torch, and the fire of revenge is spreading rapidly all over the city. I will conceal you until their wrath subsides. Go in haste to my house; my wife has all arranged Haste! I see them coming.

JEWS (*unto Jason*). Where are those men who were staying with you?

JASON. I dare not tell.

JEWS. Take him in their stead.

CAPT. (*unto Jason*). You are accused of concealing men who have turned the world upside down, teaching decrees contrary to Cæsar,—saying there is another king—(one Jesus).

JASON. You have me in your power, but those men are out of your reach.

JEWS. We will take your security for them. Remember what we say. We will have revenge.

JASON (*unto Paul and Silas*). Now brethren you must depart, for they will make every exertion to find you.

PAUL. We have concluded to go to Berea, and though we regret leaving our friends without one word of consolation, yet it would not be right to endanger your life, and ours too.

PAUL AT BEREA.

Although we have been so cordially received here, yet, I still feel anxious about the rage of those at Thessalonica.

SILAS. Oh! Brother! I see them coming rapidly.

DISCIPLE. Flee to Athens! We will be as quick to shield you, as they are to find out your whereabouts.

AT ATHENS.

EPICUREAN (*unto Paul*). What new doctrine art thou trying to establish in our midst?

STOIC. We must carry you to the Areopagus.

PAUL. I will go with pleasure, for I have heard that numbers collect there to hear or tell something new.

THE JUDGE. I would like to know the meaning of these new theories you are advancing.

[*Paul in the midst of Mars Hill.*]

Ye men of Athens: In all things I perceive you are too superstitious, for as I passed by and beheld your devotions I found you had this inscription: "To the unknown God." Whom ye therefore ignorantly worship, Him declare I unto you, God who made heaven and earth and all things therein, dwelleth not in temples made with hands, neither is He worshiped with lip service, as though He needeth anything seeing He giveth to all life and breath, and has promised that to those who seek Him, that He will be found of them, for in Him we live, and move, and have our being,—as certain of your poets have said. For we are also His offspring. Forasmuch as we are the offspring, we ought not to think the God head, is like unto gold, or silver, or stone, graven by man's device. God commands man every where to repent, because He hath appointed a day in which He will judge the world in righteousness, by that Just One whom He hath ordained, whereof He hath given assurance unto all men, in that He hath raised Him from the dead.

STOICS. We thought it would end in something about the resurrection of the dead.

EPICUREAN. We will hear you again of this matter.

DIONYSIUS. Others and myself believe, and will ever revert to this day, as the most pleasant of our lives.

PAUL AT CORINTH.

Speaketh unto the Jews. I have testified unto you that Jesus was the Christ, and ye have blasphemed and opposed me, from henceforth I will go unto the Gentiles.

CRISPUS—*Ruler of the Synagogue*—*(unto Paul).* My whole household believe, and desire to be baptized; and Justus has embraced thy cause.

[*Paul, alone in the darkness of night, heareth the Lord, saying:*]

" Be not afraid, but speak and hold not thy peace, for I am with thee, and no man shall harm thee, for I have much people in this city.

[*Paul brought before Gallio.*]

JEWS. This man persuaded men contrary to the law.

GALLIO. If there was an accusation of wickedness, I could better bear with you. But if it is a question of manners and words, and you are actuated by envy, depart at once.

PAUL (*unto Gallio*). Most Noble Gallio:—You have the honor of being the first officer, who has treated me with any degree of kindness. I have been hurled from all with "Away, with that blasphemer!" without any investigation of the charges brought against me. Accept my thanks, and you shall have my prayers and gratitude. How it cheers my heart to see I am not spurned by all, and that there is one at least who will not swerve from duty when the masses are against him.

AT EPHESUS. .

DISCIPLE. There are many here who believe, and have heard of the miracles you perform, and how you cast out devils. Last week the sons of Sceva commanded an evil spirit—by Jesus whom Paul preached. The spirit came out of the man, and possessed them, and they fell from the house wounded. The spirit said: "Jesus I know, and Paul too, but who are ye?" Great fear has fallen on all the Jews, and many have confessed, and those who used curious arts, have burned their books openly.

PAUL. May all such share the same fate. God's word will prevail. Hark! what noise is that I hear? They cry, "Great is Diana of the Ephesians." Look, they have Gaius and Aristarchus—your companions, and now they go like madmen to the theatre.

PAUL. I must go.

DISCIPLE. You know they will stone you. They have Alexander. Ah! I see it is the work of one Demetrius, who makes gold and silver shrines for Diana. He thinks his gains will be lost, and he has caused this tumult among those who are of the same opinion. List! the town clerk is now speaking, and says he will hold them responsible for so great a stir, without a cause; only a set of workmen saying it is disagreeable to them.

PAUL. I will now visit all of the disciples as the crowd has dispersed.

AT TROAS.

(*Unto the Brethren*). We must have preaching to-night. I am compelled to leave to-morrow.

[*Paul in the Synagogue.*]

DISCIPLE. There has been a death in our midst. A young man, named Eutychus, went to sleep, and fell to the first story."

PAUL. Do not be distressed ; he has signs of life.

MOTHER OF EUTYCHUS. Thou hast divine power to restore my dead son. I will ever praise God for His goodness.

AT EPHESUS.

[*Sendeth for the Church.*]

PAUL. Ye know from the first day I came unto you how I have acted, serving the Lord with humility and many tears and temptations, and how often the Jews have laid wait for me. I taught publicly, and from house to house, testifying, both to the Jews and Greeks, repentance toward our Lord Jesus Christ. And now I go bound in the spirit to Jerusalem, not knowing the things which shall befall me there, save that the Holy Ghost witnesseth, in every city that bonds and afflictions await me. Neither count I myself worthy to suffer for one who has done so much for me. I know that there are many here who shall see my face no more, therefore, I wish you would bear me record, that I am pure from the blood of all men, for I

have declared faithfully unto you the gospel of God. Be careful to feed the church of God, which has been purchased by
His blood. I know that after I depart grievous wolves will
enter in, not sparing the flock ; men shall arise and speak per-
verse things, to draw others after them. Watch therefore, and
remember that for twelve years I ceased not to warn you, both
night and day with tears. I have administered unto my own
wants—have told you that the strong ought to bear with the
weak, and that it is more blessed to give than to receive. We
will kneel and pray, before I leave. Weep not ; these earthly
separations will only be for a while, but there is a future, oh !
thank God, where the sting of parting will be felt no more.

DISCIPLES. We will go to the ship with you.

PAUL AT PTOLEMAIS.

PAUL. We must spend some time with Philip.

. PHILIP. I see Agabus, the prophet of Judea, coming. I do
hope he will prevail on you to remain with us, and not go to
Jerusalem.

[*Agabus taketh Paul's girdle and bindeth himself.*]

AGABUS. Look at me, Brother Paul ! Listen to what the
Holy Ghost says : "So shall the Jews bind at Jerusalem the
man who owns this girdle, and shall deliver him to the Gentiles."

PAUL. I know trouble awaiteth me at Jerusalem. My
friends, do not weep and break my heart. I am not only ready
to be bound for thy Saviour, but to die.

AT JERUSALEM.

[*With Disciples.*]

DISCIPLE. We are delighted to have you with us again, yet
we tremble lest evil shall befall you.

PAUL. I have good tidings from the Gentiles ; many believe,
and some are anxious to embrace the truth.

DIS. Yes, there are thousands of the Jews converted, too.
We have four men purifying themselves in the temple, would
it not be best for you to purify yourself with them, to show the
Jews you are not averse to their customs ?

Jews of Asia see Paul in the Temple, and cry:

Men of Israel, Help! This is the man who teacheth the people contrary to our law, and furthermore, hath brought Greeks into the temple to pollute it.

JEWS. Drag him out of the temple, do not defile it with his blood—beat him to death.

OFFICER (*unto Captain*). All Jerusalem is in an uproar, and they are murdering Paul.

OFFICER. Collect soldiers and centurions and go as quick as possible.

CAPTAIN (*unto Jews*). I can discover naught save your confused cries, he has done nothing worthy of death. Take him to the castle.

MULTITUDE. Away with him!

PAUL (*On the stair-case of the castle*). May I speak unto thee?

CAPT. Canst thou speak Greek? Art thou not that Egyptian who commanded four thousand murderers in the wilderness?

PAUL. I am a Jew of Tarsus, a city of Celicia, and I beseech thee to let me speak unto these people.

[*Paul stilleth the multitude and speaketh in Hebrew*]:

Men and Brethren—Hear ye my defense: I was brought up at the feet of Gamaliel, and taught according to the perfect manner of the laws of the fathers, and was zealous, as you all are. I persecuted unto death both men and women. Your High Priests can bear me witness that I obtained letters from them to bring all from Damascus to Jerusalem to be punished. And it came to pass, as I was near Damascus, about noon, suddenly there shone a bright light about me, and I fell to the ground, and heard a voice, saying: "Saul! Saul! Why persecutest thou me?" And I answered, "Who art thou, Lord?" And He said, "I am Jesus of Nazareth, whom thou persecutest." I asked, "What shall I do, Lord?" He said, "Arise, and go unto Damascus, and it shall be told thee what to do." Ananias, a devout man, was sent to tell me that I must bear witness unto all men of what I had seen and heard, and I arose and was baptized. And it came to pass again, when I was praying in the temple in Jerusalem, I was in a trance, and Christ said, "Make haste and get thee down to Jerusalem;" and I said, "Lord, they know how I have treated those who believed on Thee; and when the blood of Thy martyr Stephen was spilt I assisted." Then the Lord said, "Depart! I will send thee to the Gentiles."

MULTITUDE. Away! with this man from the earth. He can not live.

CAPTAIN. Bring him unto the house, and examine him by scourging.

PAUL. Is it lawful to bind or scourge a Roman uncondemned?

CAPT. Art thou a Roman?

PAUL. Yes.

CAPT. With a great sum obtained I this freedom.

PAUL. I was *born free!*

CAPT. (*Aside*). I regret binding him.

CAPT. To-morrow the Chief Priests and all the Council will meet, and you must appear before them for trial.

PAUL. I will be pleased to do so.

PAUL IN THE PRESENCE OF THE COUNCIL.

Men and Brethren:—I have lived in all good conscience before God until this day.

ANANIAS. Smite him on the mouth.

PAUL. God shall smite thee, thou whited wall. Sittest thou to judge me after the law, and commandest thou me to be smitten contrary to the law?

JEW. Revilest thou God's High Priests?

PAUL. I wist not, brethren, that he was a High Priest, for it is written. "Thou shalt not speak evil of thy people's ruler." Listen. I am a Pharisee! Of the hope of the resurrection of the dead, am I called in question.

PHARISEES. We find no evil in this man; and if an angel hath spoken to him, let us not fight against God.

CAPT. Bring him into the castle, or he will be torn to pieces. They are divided, and know not what they do.

The Lord speaketh at night to Paul. Be of good cheer, for as thou hast testified of me in Jerusalem, so must thou bear witness of me in Rome.

[*Paul's nephew calleth for Chief Captain.—Both enter at private room.*]

NEPHEW. I am sent to notify you that there are forty men who have taken an oath that they would neither eat, nor drink, until they had slain Paul. They intend requesting you to bring him down to-morrow to inquire more concerning him, and then they will kill him.

CAPT. See thou tell no man of this.

CAPT. (*unto Centurion*). Make ready two hundred soldiers, and horsemen three score and ten; spearsmen, two hundred. Be prepared to start by the third hour of the night. I wish to send Paul safe to Felix.

SOLDIERS (*to Paul*). We are ready. All things must be done quietly, for we will have trouble if discovered. Fear not; we will take you safe to Felix.

SOLDIERS AT CESAREA.

SOLDIER. Most Noble Felix: Here is a letter from Claudius, and a prisoner—the noted Paul.

FELIX (*unto Paul*). Claudius has found nothing worthy of death or bonds, and has therefore sent you unto me. When thy accusers come, then I can hear thee.

ANANIAS THE HIGH PRIEST, AND TERTULLUS THE ORATOR.

TERTULLUS. Most Noble Felix:—Thou art renowned for thy learning, and good judgment, and the nation feels gratified with thy wise counsel. But not desirous to be tedious unto thee, I pray that thou wouldst hear a few words: We have found this man a pestilent fellow, a ringleader of the Nazarenes, who have profaned our Holy Temple, whom we took and would have judged according to our law, but the Chief Captain Lysias took him by force, commanding his accusers to come unto thee.

JEWS. His testimony is ours.

FELIX. Paul, thou canst speak for thyself.

PAUL. Knowing that thou hast been a ruler, for many years, I do the more cheerfully answer for myself. It has been only twelve days since I went to Jerusalem to worship. They neither found me in the temple disputing with any one, or raising a disturbance in the city, or synagogue. But I do confess after the manner they call heresy, so worship I the God of my fathers, believing all things which are written in the law and prophets; and have hope towards God, which they also allow, that there shall be a resurrection of the dead. I have a conscience void of offense toward God and man. After many

years I came to bring alms to my nation, whereupon certain
Jews from Asia found me purified in the temple, neither with
multitude, nor with tumult, who ought to have been here, if they
have aught against me. But those who are here cannot say they
have found evil against me—except it be in my believing in the
resurrection of the dead.

FELIX. When Lysias comes, I will hear the utmost of the
matter.

[*Paul reasons of truth and righteousness.*]

FELIX (*trembles and says*): Go thy way for this time, at a more
convenient season I will call for thee.

PAUL (*before Festus*). These numerous complaints which the
Jews have laid before you—they cannot prove If I have done
anything worthy of death—I refuse not to die; I appeal unto
Cæsar.

FESTUS. Thou hast appealed unto Cæsar, unto Cæsar thou
shalt go.

FESTUS (*unto Agrippa*). There are accusations against
Paul, but they are prompted wholly by the superstition of the
Jews.

AGRIPPA. I would like to hear him myself.

PAUL BEFORE FESTUS AND AGRIPPA.

FESTUS. Here is the man whom prejudice says ought not to
live any longer, and as he has appealed unto Cæsar, I would like
to know what charges to send with him. Therefore, I would be
pleased if you would examine him, most noble Agrippa.

AGRIPPA. Paul, thou art permitted to speak for thyself.

PAUL. I think myself happy, King Agrippa, that I may
answer concerning all the things whereof I am accused by the
Jews, and I do beseech thee to hear me patiently. My manner
of life from my youth—all know, and how many saints I shut up
in prison. And as I was going to Damascus, I saw a light at
midday, above the brightness of the sun; and I heard a voice,
saying: "Saul! Saul! Why persecutest thou me?" And I
said: "Who art thou, Lord?" The Voice said: "I am Jesus
whom thou persecutest. I will make thee a minister, and a
witness of these things which will appear unto thee. Whereupon oh! King Agrippa, I was not disobedient to the heavenly
vision. But shewed first unto them of Damascus, and at Jerusalem, and to the Gentiles, that they should repent, and turn to
God. For these causes alone the Jews caught me in the temple

and intended to kill me, but I had help from God, and still witness to small and great, none other things than those which Moses and the prophets did say should come to pass—that Christ should suffer and be raised from the dead, and should be a light unto the Gentiles.

FESTUS. Paul, thou art beside thyself; much learning doth make thee mad.

PAUL. I am not mad, most noble Felix, but speak forth the words of truth and soberness. The king knoweth of these things, for they were not done in a corner. King Agrippa, believest thou the prophets? I know that thou believest?

AGRIPPA. Almost thou persuadest me to be a Christian.

PAUL. I would to God that not only thou, but also those who are with thee—were not almost, but were altogether such as I am—save these bonds.

KING (aside unto Bernice). This man doeth nothing worthy of death.

AGRIPPA. If thou hadst not appealed unto Cæsar, thou couldst have been free Hope you will have a pleasant journey to Italy.

PAUL. Thank you. The kindness I have met with here, will ever be an oasis in the desert of my memory.

PAUL ON BOARD THE VESSEL.

JULIAS (to Paul). When we land, you can visit your relatives and friends.

PAUL. We are near the Fair Havens. I fear this voyage will be one of peril to our lives, and destruction to the ship.

CAPT. The harbor is not commodious to winter in. We must go to Phenice; we have a south wind, and will soon make it.

PAUL. It has only been a few hours since I told you to beware, and ye heeded not. Now the Euroclydon is blowing, and we will have trouble.

CAPT. Have the ship undergirded, I fear we will be dashed against the quicksands. This is the third day since we have seen the sun, or stars.

SOLDIERS. We will be lost! All must have a watery grave.

CAPT. I have done all in my power; this noble barque has fought long and bravely against the angry waves, but she will soon be dashed to pieces

PAUL. Sirs, you should have listened to me, and not loosed from Crete. But be of good cheer, there shall be no loss of life—only the grand old ship, and she is now making her dying struggles.

CAPT. Oh! Paul! Thou art a man of God, and I do repent not taking heed to thy advice; do tell me how thou knowest we will be saved.

PAUL. There stood by me to night an angel of God, whom I serve, and said: "Fear not, Paul, thou must be brought before Cæsar. And Lo! God hath given thee all who sail with thee." Now, be of good cheer, for it will be as God has promised, yet we must be cast on a certain island.

CAPT. I think we are near land; have them to see.

PAUL. We had best cast anchor and wait for the morning.

SAILORS. We will risk our lives in the deep—this vessel cannot last an hour longer.

PAUL (unto Centurion). Unless these men stay in the ship they cannot be saved—and this is the fourteenth day we have been fasting, and you all must eat something, for no harm shall befall any of you. Now let us give thanks, and believe that the three score and sixteen souls shall be saved.

CAPT. Throw the wheat overboard. I see land, and we must thrust the ship into the creek. Ah! noble vessel! We must soon bury thee beneath the waves, with which thou hast battled so bravely! Would that we could save thee, for we have watched with breathless anxiety thy peaceful movements when the waves seemed like playthings to thee. But now, thou art mastered. I see the hinder part of the ship is broken! Do all you can to save yourselves.

SOLDIERS. Would it not be best to kill the prisoners, lest some of them escape?

CENTURION. No, not one life shall be taken! All who can swim, cast yourselves into the sea and try to make the land. Here are boards and planks, for those who cannot swim.

PAUL. Do not be alarmed! Be of good cheer! All I have told you has come to pass, so far. I know we shall all be saved.

SOLDIER. Catch my arm, I am sinking.

PAUL. Here is a stick; be composed. Now you are safe, help others.

CAPT. (to Paul). We will consider you a prophet, and must say there is a reality in the religion you profess. They are all

safe. Let us go to the fire and warm, it is kind of these strangers to anticipate our wants.

PAUL. I will take some wood with me.

CAPT. Oh! snake! Knock it off. Ah! it is too late! You
are bitten! Are you suffering much?

PAUL. I feel no pain at all.

BARBARIAN. We thought this man must have been a murderer, and though he escaped the storm, was doomed to die a
more painful death. But now we see he is not hurt, and conclude he is a god! or he would have fallen dead. The bite of
this serpent is always fatal.

PAUL. The God whom I serve has spared me. It is from Him
alone I look for help. I can do nothing of myself.

PUBLIUS (*Ruler of the Island*). I want you to remain with us
as loug as you can be contented.

PAUL. Thank you. We did not expect such hospitality from
strangers.

PUBLIUS. My father is very sick, and I believe you possess
power from on high, so I wish you would come and see him.

PAUL. I have naught, save what my Father giveth me.

BARBARIAN. There is something mysterious about this man.
He only laid his hands on the father of Publius, and he recovered: and he has healed many others. The soldiers say he
foretold them of their danger. Have you seen him?

BARBARIAN. No. I wish he would remain with us. He is
not like other men—will receive no credit for what he does.

PAUL AT ROME.

PAUL (*before the Jews*). Men and Brethren:--Though I have
committed nothing against the people, or their customs, yet was
I delivered prisoner from Jerusalem, into the hands of the
Romans, who when they had examined me, would have let me
go, not finding anything worthy of death in me. But when the
Jews spake against it, I appealed unto Cæsar. Not that I had
aught to accuse my nation of, but to say that for the hope of
Israel, I am bound with this chain.

JEWS. We have not heard anything of your imprisonment,
and welcome you in our midst. We desire to hear you speak,
and wish you to dwell some time with us.

ANOTHER PARTY OF JEWS. He said that our eyes were

closed, and our ears dull of hearing, and we would not understand with our hearts, that we may be converted, and that he
was sent to the Gentiles.

PAUL. Brethren, my past history you all know. I expect to
remain two years with you. If we are united, we can march as
one great phalanx against the enemy. There must be no vain
strife, but all work together in God's grand army, having Jesus
for our Captain. And when we lay our armor down, each can
say: "I have fought a good fight.—The battle is over, and now
I will rest in peace!"

LINES

WRITTEN AFTER THE DEATH OF MY BABE.

My bud of innocence, thou wilt bloom above
Amidst the songs of angels, and a Saviour's love.
No sigh will ever rend thine infant breast,
Nor tear bedim thine eye ; thou art at rest.
Strike the harp gently in thy blissful home ;
Let Mother catch the echo, till she come
To clasp thee to her loving heart,
Of which for aye thou art alone the larger part.
Oh Birdie, thou did'st nestle near
Thy mother. What hadst thou to fear ?
Pure as a dew drop on the lily's leaf,
Thou'rt gone ! Thy mother's heart is filled with grief.
Oh God ! is it because I am of sinner's chief ?
Father of heaven, I pray thee send to me relief.
List ! I hear a sweet voice from out the skies :
Brush the tear-drop from thine aching eyes,
The family chain is broken--this link of love,
Will gently draw thee to thy home above.

→✳ MORNING REVERIE.. ✳←

Hark! Listen! What is that I hear? It is the matin lay
Of Nature's warblers, joining glad, to wake the drowsy day.
Lift up your heads, ye flow'rets fair besprinkled o'er with dew,
And hail the joyous hour of morn with fragrance rich and new.
Leap high and dash your snowy foam, ye silvery wimpling rills,
And make soft music as ye wend your way down wooded hills;
Aurora's herald streaks will fade in growing light of day,
The sun, like monarch waked from sleep, will brighten with his
    ray
The upland slope, the meadow green, the field of waving corn,
And of his genial smile, erstwhile, a thousand beauties born,
Will gladden with a heavenly thrill all Nature's vast expanse,
And happiness of bird and rill a thousand-fold enhance.
Oh, dullard man! unheeding all! Awake thee from thy slumber,
And to the Giver of all good raise thou the tuneful number;
All these for thee did God create; lead thou the joyful measure,
And let not brook and field, innate, proclaim thy shameful
    leisure.
Come forth in grandeur and in might, a son of light and power,
With mind and soul equipped for good, to meet the labor hour.
The harvest all about you lies, who will the sheaflets bind
With earnest zeal and rock ribbed faith, and loving, willing
    mind,
For the home on high, where angels are, and bliss abides for
    aye--
Where the crown for the cross, the harp for the hook, for life
    the undimmed eye?
Arouse, arouse! ye sons of men! The conflict now is fierce,
'Tis hand to hand, and sword to sword, if we the ranks would
    pierce,
And drive the foe from out the field, whose presence is our
    shame;--
Relying in our greatest need on the Almighty Name,
Whose prevalence must conquer all, and make us victors, too.
He will our courage, strength and joy, from day to day renew;
We'll trust us to His strong Right arm, through which we'll
    surely win--
Prayer is the door to heaven's joys, Faith the key to let us in.

→✳ EVOLUTION. ✳←

ITS ADVOCATES.—THE PYRAMID.

THE spirit of Evolution is diffusing itself in our schools, permeating our literature, and attempting to undermine the Bible I would not have the egotism to differ with the scientific men of the age, if I did not have the testimony of the most noted geologist in direct contradiction to what they affirm. Prof. Dana, of Yale College, says on page 262 of his Geology: "The man ape nearest in structure to man, has a cranium of but thirty-four cubits in capacity — or half that of the lowest existing man; and no link between has been found—no human remains that the past fifteen years of active research have brought to light, afford evidence of the existence of a race less perfectly erect than the man, or nearer to the man-ape in essential characteristics." The man-ape of the present day—the Gorilla, the Orang-outang — are the termination of the lines of succession that reaches up to them; but as to the line supposed to end in man, not the first link has been found. Thus geological discovery leaves man alone at the head of the system of life, far removed from his nearest allies among the brute creation.

On page 238 of the same book, he speaks of the skulls and skeletons of man, being found in the southern part of France, and in Belgium, which will compare with any of the present day. Prof. Dana also answered through the *New York Independent*, in this impressive language: " I further endeavor to show that man's physical nature, as well as his spiritual, was not the product, or educt of evolutionary processes, but it demanded for its creation a divine act, referring for proof (as done by Wallace) to Huxley, who says that the brain of the lowest race of man, has twice the cubic contents of the man-ape; and further to the fact, that the skeleton of man is adapted throughout for a vertical position, and that of an ape for an inclined one." And that geology has discovered no human remains anywhere, that indicate a lower grade of man than now exists, or one that makes the first shade of approximation to the inclined structure of the ape, and also to the existence of a moral sense,

all showing that some other power than nature's, was required
for man's production."

I quote so extensively from Dana, because every school boy
and girl is conversant with his Geology; and I write for them,
and wish to impress it upon their minds, that this is not the
language of a feeble-minded woman—but of such men as Dana,
Wallace and Huxley. Yet the advocates of Evolution tell us
they get their knowledge from Geology, and many of the would-
be scientific, swallow this morsel of infidelity without even
chewing it. But my young friends, I want you to analyze every
part carefully, before you even taste of this tempting bait.
Now I wish you to listen to one of the brightest lights in the
Evolutionary horizon. Though a believer, he does not wish to
delude others. He says, in the *Scientific Monthly*: "That mere
reasoning can never convince the world. It must be hard, de-
fiant facts, which none can gainsay. But verily no such facts,
nor even their most distant forecasts, are before us. The
profound difficulties which bustle round the inquiry, on every
hand, are prominent signals for caution, while the uncertainty
and incompetency of the methods hitherto employed, and their
conflicts of results, is alive with meaning. We know from
actual observation almost nothing with certainty, and the little
we do know from such careful and patient observers as Cohen,
Billroth, Lancaster, Ray and others, is so complex and conflicting as to demonstrate the necessity of years of patient experi-
ment, and skillful research, to plainly tell us of our ignorance.
The largest difficulty surrounding the question of the mode
of origin of sceptic organisms, is that of discovering the life
cycle. By dealing with them in aggregations, we run told and
untold risks. The conflict of results by this means, in the most
accomplished hands, employing the most refined methods,
during the past eighteen years, is sufficient witness. Repeti-
tions of experiments and conflicting results, and explanations
of the reasons why—and so the cycle rolls. Of course, important lessons are learned; but not *the* lesson. For the weight
of evidence is not only, not in favor of abiogenesis, but in the
strongest sense adverse to it. This great man (Dallinger)
wants the truth, and nothing but the truth. Would that all
were equally honest, then the monument would be removed,
and the putrefying body of infidelity unearthed. The president
of Princeton College, after proving the impossibility of agnos
ticism, asks, if we believe in this system what have we left, to

cheer us through life, or to cling to in death ? Will we be apt to
set a higher value on life when we know it to be a mere bundle
of impressions, with unsubstantial ideas growing out of them ?
Will we take a deeper interest in our neighbors when we have
come to believe theoretically (for to believe it practically is im-
possible) that they too are mere congeries of appearances ?
Will we be disposed to do more for the world when we regard
it as a set and series of phantasmagoria, bound by rigid uni-
formities of likeness, co-existence and succession ? Will we
be most likely to feel that life is worth living, and that it is our
duty to work for its good, when we contemplate it as a mere
series of images, which do not reflect any reality ? Will not
one hindrance to self-indulgence be removed when we are made
to acknowledge that sensations and pleasures are realities, and
that there are no others ? Will not one hindrance to self-murder
which we may be tempted to commit when in trouble, be removed, when we are sure that we are merely stopping a series
of sensations ? Will the regret of the learned murderer be
deepened, when he is told by the highest philosophy that he has
only put an arrest on a few pulsations ? Agnosticism can never
become the creed of the great mass of any people, but if it
should be taught by the philosophy of the day, I fear its influence on the youth, who might be led, not to amuse themselves
with it, but by faith to adopt it, and would find some of the
hindrances to vice removed, and some of the incentives to evil
encouraged. It destroys the foundation of all religions, and
those w ho receive such a system must prepare themselves to
part with all the consolation they ever received from religion.
Now, weigh well what you have read. The testimony of the
first man is, that important lessons in Biology have been
learned—but not *the* lesson—and that after eighteen years of
patient research, there has not been found one link to connect
the iron chain of reasoning. And what has been learned are mere
signals for caution. Then the president of Princeton College,
uniting his voice with thousands of others, warning the youth
of our land to beware of the quagmire of infidelity, which so
many of them are rushing madly into.

But if there was not one man who had moral courage enough
to speak one word against Evolution, there is a monument, the
echo of whose voice has sounded through forty centuries, saying to the scientific of to-day, "I look down with disdain upon
this progressive age ; I transcend by fifty feet the pinnacles of

St. Peter at Rome; I am the most accurately oriented building in the world; my foundation covers thirteen acres of ground; the immense blocks of stone of which I am built are eight feet in length, nearly the same in breadth, and five feet in thickness; these rise in tiers, one above the other, comprising two hundred and sixty layers, making my height four hundred and eighty-four feet. How these stones were quarried, adjusted, and by what machinery lifted, defies the best engineers of the present day to answer. I have witnessed the ruin of many empires, yet remained silent for four thousand years, but now I will utter forth the voice of God in lofty eloquence, and unfold the prophecies of His Word, asking the atheistic world to unravel the mathematical and astronomical labyrinths of knowledge possessed by the semi-brutes of the transition period. The Royal Astronomer of Scotland, Prof. Smyth, will explain why I was built. Joseph Taylor Goodsir, F. R. S. E., asserts that sound science is not only a handmaid, but a defender of sound religion, and brings my adamantine materials to testify to the state of the stellar heavens at the time of my building. I help to determine the date of the flood, and to give consistency to the chronology and history of diluvian and post-diluvian times. I testify to the importance of the physical sciences, terrestrial and cosmical, not merely from the utilitarian, but from a religious point of view. We thus see united, science and religion, testifying from my summit, with re-awakened voice, just as they were intended to do more than four thousand years ago. I am the oldest building, and I harmonize with the oldest book. St. John, Vincent Day, civil engineer of Glasgow, and numbers of others speak of me in a similar manner. And it appears to me the most absurd of all theories, that men just emerging from monkeyhood, could understand the science of the heavens and earth, better than those of this advanced age.

God made man a powerful and highly intellectual being, but some of them feel their degeneracy so keenly, they conclude they must be nearly related to some brute. "But I stand here in my massive strength, testifying to the world that it required more science than Evolutionists possess to build me, and when I am properly understood I will cause the advocates of this blighting system to stagger with the weight of their own convictions. And my voice will be heard when the brutalizing atheism of this progressive age lies buried by its infidel brothers, Porphyry, Julian, Voltaire, Hume and Bolingbroke.

⇥✳ TO MY THOUGHTLESS CHILDREN. ✳⇤

MY heart is sad to-night.
 Oh! lamps, why shine so bright?
 As if in mockery of my fears,
E'en stars refuse to watch my tears.
Terrific clouds are gathering fast,
Night's dark shrouds are o'er me cast;
The angry waves do foam and dash;
Thunders roar, and lightnings flash;
Still my children have not come.
What would life be? What would home?
Did not their presence chase the gloom!
Despair would soon my life entomb.
Ah! my prayers seem all in vain,
And my heart must burst with pain.
Stop my children! Pause and think!
You perchance are on the brink
Of death's dark flood; 'tis cold and wide,
And deep! Without a Saviour's guide
You ne'er can stem this raging flood.
Your strength lies only in His blood.
On bended knee, for mercy cry.
The Lord will hear, nor will deny
His boat of life to yonder shore,
Where sting of death is felt no more.

.

➤✳ THE LAST WORDS ✳◄

OF A CONFEDERATE SOLDIER.

COUSIN! the tide of life is ebbing fast,
And the gates of death will soon be past.
Come now, and kneel close by my side,
And list as life doth switly glide.
Thou hast shared with me my grief and joys;
We've known and loved since we were boys.
Do you remember one bright spring-like day?
When the birds sang sweetest in the month of May?
How we gathered our hats full of lovely flowers,
And chased the butterflies for many hours ?
There played with us a little girl, with dark brown hair,
And eyes, and rosy, dimpled cheeks, and skin so fair.
We gathered shells on the sea-beach strand,
And I read your mind, as you traced on sand,
Lines to one you loved.   Since then her name
Has ever been your theme, and guiding star to fame.
Alas! our childhood's gone, our years have flown.
We little boys have now to manhood grown.
What's that we hear? our gun's call! the band!
Blood has been spilt!   Distress is o'er our land!
Strong hearts must break at this the parting hour.
The die is cast, and storm-clouds o'er us lower.
There is a being, pure—a noble lover's pride,
Soon to become his lovely, childish bride.
Then hearts will bleed at war's stern blast,
And brightest hopes be relegated to the past.
Well do I remember on that eve serene,
The tears and sadness of that parting scene.
You thought you felt the keenest pang,
For with much gaiety I talked and sang.
But there was smothered flame, a fire
Consumed my heart.   I feared that ire
Would take the place of brother's love.
I tell thee all, for soon above

The trials of this mocking life
I sweet shall rest from passion's strife.
Tell her—my life I laid on my country's shrine.
My last wish was, she should be thine.
I'd fain have her weep, with drooping head,
When you return with glad and gallant tread,
For I shall live, though numbered with the dead.
Live with my Lord. Death has no dread.
With leagued oppression poured by northern hate,
I shudder for my friends, but may their fate
Be that of Spartan bold, and Thermopylæ,
Their watchword ever, Death or Liberty!
For I would rather fill an honored soldier's grave,
Than crouch to Tyranny—a conquered slave.
Of those at home, I would now like to speak,
Raise my head--Some water. Ah! so weak.
This lock of hair I send my aged mother.
My sword I so cherished, to my oldest brother.
Tell them, upheld by faith I do not fear:
Christ is my surety; my release is near.
More air! Water! Oh! this anguished breath.
Farewell friends! farewell! The soldier lay in death.

→✳ THE OLD GRAPEVINE. ✳←

PAPA, spare that lovely vine.
　My heart will ever round it twine.
　Don't tear it from its rustic home,
It cares not for a costly dome.

Oft my play-house I have made,
And laid my dolls beneath its shade.
Who would not love this fairy bower,
Where life seemed but one joyous hour!

Well do I remember many a time,
Of stealing grapes from this aged vine,
While the other children would jump with glee,
And say, "Throw them down! Papa wont see."

Its tendrils doth around me cling,
And 'neath its shade I often sing.
I've watched it bear for six long years,
It 's heard my laugh and seen my tears.

Then, Papa, do not scorn my tear,
Though weak to you it may appear.
But spare for me this aged vine,
Whose tendrils round my heart-strings twine.

➤✻ GEORGE ELIOT : ✻←

HER MORAL CHARACTER, AND THE ANTI-CHRISTIAN TENDENCY OF HER WRITINGS.

I would not treat departed eminence with disrespect, but in analyzing all characters of note, it is a duty to separate the gold from the dross; lest while we are profusely embalming the dead with eulogisms, we ensnare the living into a net of admiration, from which they cannot easily extricate themselves.

The unmixed commendation of George Eliot's talents, without the most gentle censure of her principles and practices, will impress the youthful mind with over-valuation of genius, unsanctified by Christian principles, or dignified by virtuous conduct.

No brilliancy of mind or diversity of attainments should ever be allowed as commutation for defective morals, or corrupt ideas. And George Eliot did prepare a solution of poison which she sedulously diffused through her writings, knowing that it would be more universally fatal than the elixir of her friends Tyndal, Spencer and Huxley, whose automaton she was. The fascinating label of romance would cause the indolent thinkers to taste, while only an industrious few would attempt to analyze the compounds of biology, sociology, and paleontology. These glittering threads of romance which she interweaves in the texture of her infidelity, charm even the lowest of minds. She attempts to annihilate chastity, by making her heroes and heroines appear more remarkable and amiable without it, thus alluring the unsuspecting to embrace vice—not that they prefer it, but because she has it so masked as to represent virtue. This plausible, metaphysical sophistry debauches the very core of virtue; and, like the deadly mildew, blights the blooming promise of the spring of life. She makes her heroes and heroines descant on depravity with as much solemnity as if their object was to allay the tumult of the passions, while they are letting them loose by plucking off the muzzle of present restraint and future accountableness. This bold impiety and brutish sensuality will wrap fatally about the heart, and check its moral circulation, and totally stop the pulse of goodness; or, in other words, it will choke the stream of virtue, by drying up the fountain of future remorse and remote repentance.

Some may say, as Schopenhauer and Hartmann, that morals and religion are necessary for the masses. But the sun of genius will shed a halo so bright, that even licentiousness will be overshadowed.

Mary Clemmer and others who say that George Eliot's moral nature was too seraphic to be commented on by common people, are but echoing the voice of Sandoval, when he declared the profligate Alexander, of the house of Medici, to be a person of excellent manners, and although he acknowledges his licentiousness, Sandoval makes him so fascinating that he charmed those Florentines, whose dukedom he had usurped, and whose wives and daughters he had dishonoured. Another in speaking of the Medici, says: "Their having restored knowledge and elegance will in time obliterate their faults. Their usurpation, tyranny, pride, perfidy, and incest, will be remembered no more. Future generations will forget their atrocious crimes, in fond admiration." Is not this the prevailing sentiment which encircles the memory of George Eliot? Some may think this dark shading for so bright a picture ; and it is with feelings of regret that I have thus to deface what might have thrilled all with delight. But there is a secluded spot on the landscape, which is but seldom seen. Look at that lone cypress tree—beneath its dark shades sits a woman in deep distress! Hear her cries of anguish, as she drops a half-opened letter, exclaiming, "My husband has forsaken me! Forgotten those sacred vows he uttered in the presence of God and man! My hands are cold, and my heart throbs with pain! Oh! let me be hurled—anywhere! Anywhere! out of the world!" When we ask who is this? some one whispers, Mrs. Lewes, the heart-broken wife of the man who once traveled over Europe and America with George Eliot. Yet this star, whose radiance every woman might have delighted to bask in, darkly excluded every ray of hope from an innocent and lawful wife. And shall we palliate such turpitude? Or countenance that crime which cuts up order and virtue by the roots, and violates the sanctity of happiness to many homes ? God forbid that the women of the United States should ever lower their standard of right, though a Sarah Bernhardt should fascinate with her art, and a George Eliot charm with her talents. With feelings of pride we view the Parnassian territory which the former is now invading, and the latter has occupied. Yet we must regret that the purity of their hearts has not eclipsed the brilliancy of their minds.

→✳ "THERE IS NO HARM IN IT." ✳←

THERE are few lovers of pleasure who have not made use of this phrase, and its alluring appearance, masked with innocence, has drawn more into the vortex of ruin, than any other in the English language. Few are systematically, or premeditatively wicked, or propose to themselves more than those indulgences which they are persuaded—"there is no harm in." But the expression is so vague that every one can furnish his own definition, and each one can extend the limits a little farther, until the bounds which fenced out, permitted no unlawful and unpermitted pleasures, are gradually broken-down, and all marks of them obliterated. I am satisfied there are many fashionable women and men, who are daily disseminating mischief by indulging in the dangerous notion—"that there is no harm in anything short of positive vice." Shakspeare says: "You are the makers of manners," speaking of those who occupy prominent positions in society; and if such be makers, they should be guardians of public taste and virtue. I fear too few, give this important subject the thought that is due it, or we would not hear those who guide the young, indulge in the baneful use of slang. Should not the object of conversation be to elevate rather than degrade? Is not slang superfluous, indecent and degrading? I am aware that many ladies talk in innuendoes, and if they could hear the meaning echoed back, their modesty would be shocked. For when they touch the note of slang, there are vibrations to the lowest thought in the bosoms of most men, and how often they condemn with their tongues, what they approve by their smiles! There are but few meetings where golden coins of the imagination are interchanged, like those of the gallant Sir Philip Sidney, and Sir Walter Raleigh, when they met 'neath the cool shades of their loved Mulga. Oh! would that those who indulge in slang, could see how much dross, and how little pure gold they have from each conversation. They certainly would not say there is no harm in it, because it is almost universally adopted. And the advocate for dancing will bring in a similar argument, with an appendage that it is better to dance than slander your neighbor.—This I admit, for envy is the main-spring to slander, and those who indulge in either, are like the loathsome toad which cannot pass the fairest flower without casting its filthy froth on it.

But proving that slandering is the greater of the two evils, does not by any means prove there is no harm in dancing. If you had committed homicide, would you like your lawyer to commence his defense, by asserting your crime might have been darker? Sallust, the Pagan historian of the great Roman conspirator, said that his mistress was too good a dancer to be a virtuous woman. If there is any impropriety in wasting time and talents, or in being hugged very closely, then there must be harm in dancing. You hear this fashionable amusement denounced by most church members and ministers; yet they are inconsistent enough to attend a circus, and not only encourage the most disgraceful modes of dancing, but licentiousness, both by their presence and purses. They must have a very elastic conscience to fit all occasions.

There is another fashionable evil indulged in by some of our best ladies and gentlemen. I allude to card playing, which is equally as fascinating as dancing, and a simple game of cards has often led to gambling, which is a twin brother to dissipation, and both destroy happiness and fortune. Then, if so much harm can result from a glass of wine, or a game of cards, should we not abstain from the very appearance of evil? We ought to remember that gamblers and drunkards are not born, but made, by the iron fetters of habit. There seems to be a mysterious mania in some fashionable circles, for the society of any, save wife or husband, and I believe this custom is doing more to stab domestic felicity to the heart, than any *ignis fatuus* the deluded ever followed, and is giving to the reporters those ghastly statistics.

The Examiner spoke of some time since,—one hundred and eighty-eight deaths resulting from jealousy alone. This stern fact, alarming as it is, gives the gleanings of but one reporter, and if a few of those horrible scenes which preceded those deaths, could be presented to the view of fashionable men and women, who are almost strangers around their own hearthstones, they certainly would awaken from their complacent dreams, and realize that it will only be a question of time, ere they pass through similar trials, unless they cease to apply to their consciences that fatal opiate—"There is no harm in anything which custom approves." If we could only rise superior to the illusion of fashion, and analyze every practice before we adopt it, we might so raise our characters, that we would make the next age better, and have posterity in our debt, for the advantages it will receive by our example.

➤✳ A DREAM. ✳←

ONE sultry summer night, with feverish brain,
    I tried to sleep, but all my efforts were in vain.
    Soon kind Morpheus came with soothing balm,
And gentle Zephyr helped with heavenly calm.
Then came refreshing sleep ; I did sweetly dream,
Of a far-off clime, covered in glittering sheen.
Then Spring came. I was on steps of a palace fair,
And the birds sang sweetly, 'mid flowers rare ;
When suddenly there came forth, the wheel of time
And a soft voice whispered which seemed divine :
Come with me ! for I wouldst have thee behold,
Something of the future, yet much must be untold.
Look to the right ! See the rugged hill of life,
There's not all sunshine, but often clouds and strife.
Look at the valley of Contentment, see, in it Felicity
Is graven on that lofty pillar, there's peace, and simplicity.
Midst lotus flowers, emblems of holiness, and lilies of beauty,
All are pure, godliness reigneth here, all do their duty.
Near it you see the Plain of Solitude, and 'neath its shade,
Milton's mind grew and matured, and a Cincinnatus was made.
It inspired Demosthenes, 'tis the only nurse of the great.
There, Reflection loves to dwell, and we think on our future
    state.
Look amidst that burning sea, there's Ambition's mountain ;
The spur of discontent, makes some drink of its hissing
    fountain.
Empedocles leaped into the fiery Etna, to write his name
On that glittering pinnacle which many call fame,
Yet all desire fame, and there's a kind that all commendeth,
Yes this is a laudable thirst, where peace and honor blendeth.
I see your feet are bleeding, you look languid and careworn,
You've passed through many trials, and your heart is torn
By thorns of unkindness, but that is in the eternal past ;
Christ has ever been thy guide. Now would you one look cast
Down the hill of life ? In slippery places your feet have trod,
Yet you have clung to Jesus, and will be happy with your God.
There's the dark valley of death, but look to yonder shore,
There's the haven of rest, where sin and grief are felt no more.

➤✻ THE BATTLE OF GALVESTON. ✻⬅

A S I wandered o'er the sea-beach fair,
 I heard a noise so strange and rare.
 'Twas not the splash of silver wave,
That sighs and moans over many a grave.
No ; 'twas the cannon's fitful roar,
Thundering along our lovely shore.

In breathless haste I onward sped,
Not knowing where my pathway led,
Until I stood in the battle's face,
To witness the passion of the human race.
Our forces were commanded by Magruder.
If not the purest, we have seen ruder,
For he has taken one sip at the cup of fame,
Which will ever give him an immortal name.
But to return to our subject again,
Which we can revert to without shame.

The battle was raging in the midst of night.
The firing was terrific to our sight,
Thundering of guns, as they lavished forth
Their volleys of hatred to the Isle of the South.
I thought Pluto might be venting his ire.
The waves appeared like billows of fire.

Goliah-like, the mighty ironclads
Had dared our brave and trusting lads,
To the gulf which they seemed destined to keep,
They would give their bodies to the fish of the deep.
Ah! our men waver ; they've accomplished their fete
The battle 's won and their victory is complete.

Hark! there's noise in another direction,
Lo! we have been under God's protection.
The king of the waters rides proudly on,
Not heeding the burst of the pelting storm,

Behold! he reaches the proud Harriet Lane,
The men shoot, as if they were all insane;
Their enemies waver, their column melts away,
But the Neptune is wounded and cannot stay
To rejoice. So flying to his brother near,
He parts with his men he loves so dear,
And takes his calm and glorious sleep,
'Neath the foaming waves of the briny deep

Again the enemy rally; and on deck they fly,
Vengeance beaming from every eye.
But alas, they are soon hurled below.
God is above man's vain boast and show.
Ah! they are surrendering to our noble few,
Aurora is smiling, and bespangling with dew
Our lovely flag of red, white and blue.

This proclaimed to the Venice of Texas the story,
That victory perched on her banner of glory.
Galveston was free from terror and spoil,
And blood had been spilt on Lone Star State soil.

*   *   *   *   *

Mars has called His warriors home;
They are waiting to welcome all that come
Where the cannon's roar will be heard no more,
On that calm, peaceful, celestial shore.

"The true friend is not he who holds up flattery's mirror,
    In which to thy conceit, most pleasing hovers,—
But he who shews thee all thy vices, sirrah!
    And helps to mend them ere an enemy discovers!"

⇥✳ INVOCATION ✳⇤

WRITTEN DURING THE CIVIL WAR.

OH Lord, no longer hide Thy face,
  Bless us with Thy loving grace,
  Let our prayers reach Thy throne !
Not our will, but Thine be done.
We are sinful, Thou canst forgive,
For Jesus' sake, Oh ! let us live ;
We are in the shroud of grief,
Smile again, and give relief.
List ! Hope, with her cheering voice,
Bids our aching hearts rejoice.
Man can do naught without God's power ;
Oft he fades like summer flower ;
Israel's trials came through sin,
Repentance did God's blessing win ;
Each father pities his child's distress,
Our heavenly Parent will not do less ;
Let us humble us, and kiss the dust,
And He will wipe away the rust
From our hearts, and fill with love,
For all that is good, in our home above.
Our troubles will vanish as the mist of a day,
When God shall change our night into day.

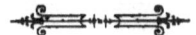

Read not to contradict, nor to believe, but to weigh, and
consider. Some books are to be tasted, others to be swallowed,
and some few to be chewed anddigested. Histories make men
wise, Poets witty, Mathematics subtile, Natural Philosophy
deep, Morals grave, Logic and Rhetoric, able to contend.

⇒✳ WISHES TO A FRIEND ✳⇐

SOON TO BE MARRIED.

I would twine for thee a garland fair,
Of lilies pure, and orange rare.
From sins dark quiver, ne'er a dart
Be sent to pierce thy trusting heart;
Nor mildew of sorrow ever blight
The roses of love. Hope light each night,
Making thy life a scene of joy,
Without the shade of sorrow's dark alloy.

*　　　　*　　　　*　　　　*　　　　*

Allow me to congratulate you upon your anticipated felicity.
And as you launch forth your boat on the matrimonial sea, may
it be plied by oars of love, and its anchor be ever that of Hope.
May it gently glide down the stream of life. But if the storm of
adversity should ever darken thy sky, and the resurging waves
of disappointment dash against thy barque, may the sunshine of
godliness send forth its ray of peace, shedding over thee a halo
of happiness!

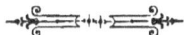

" Hence from all ages the cabinet divine
Has held high counsel over the fate of man,
Nor have the clouds those gracious counsels hid,
Angels undrew the curtains of the throne,
And Providence came forth to meet mankind."

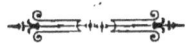

" Lean not on earth—'Twill pierce thee to the heart—
A broken reed at best—but oft a spear. On its sharp
Point, Peace bleeds, and Hope expires."

➤✳ MILLER TO BURNS. ✳◀

MIGHT you not, on yon slanting beam
 Of moonlight kneeling to the Doon,
 Descend once more, to this hallowed stream ?
Sure yon stars yield enough of light,
To spare from heaven thy face one night.

  *   *   *   *   *

The meek-eyed stars are cold and white
And steady fixed for all the years,
The comet burns the wing of night
And dazzles elements and spheres,
Then dies in beauty and a blaze,
Of light blown far through other days.

"Canute, the Danish king of England, being disgusted with
the flattery of his subjects, rebuked their folly, by commanding
his chair to be set by the edge of the water, while the tide was
rising, so that he might compel the rude waters to depart from
his dominions. But the billows heeded not his kingly commands ; whereupon he called on his servile flatterers, to remember how feeble was the sway of kings, in comparison with
the King of Kings."

Brother the boquet which thou hast given me,
Shall bloom long, and fresh in my memory ;
Nothing did so pleasantly, my hours beguile,
As the fragrance of flowers, and thy smile.

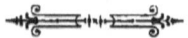

"Like our shadows, our wishes lengthen, as our sun declines".